TRULY, MADLY, FAMOUSLY

Books by Rebecca Serle

Famous in Love
Truly, Madly, Famously

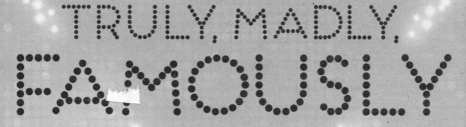

TRULY, MADLY, FAMOUSLY

A FAMOUS IN LOVE NOVEL

REBECCA SERLE

MACMILLAN

First published in the US 2015 by Poppy, an imprint of Little, Brown and Company

First published in the UK 2015 by Macmillan Children's Books
an imprint of Pan Macmillan
20 New Wharf Road, London N1 9RR
Associated companies throughout the world
www.panmacmillan.com

ISBN 978-1-4472-5037-1

1 3 5 7 9 8 6 4 2

A CIP catalogue record for this book is available from
the British Library.

Printed and bound by CPI Group (UK) Ltd, Croydon CR0 4YY

For my sister, Yfat Reiss Gendell.
There are no outs. Now it's in writing

Fame is a bee.

It has a song

It has a sting

Ah, too, it has a wing.

—Emily Dickinson

"They are the hunters, we are the foxes. And we run."

—Taylor Swift

CHAPTER 1

LAX. Post fifteen hours of travel. Dried skin. Swollen ankles. Sunglass-covered dark-circled eyes. It's no one's sexiest look, yet it's the one that gets photographed more than any other. I don't know why a single soul would want to see me like this. But they must. Because every time I get off a plane at least thirty-five people are standing outside to photograph me. And the pictures will land everywhere. My rumpled jeans and matted hair will be splashed across every single tabloid the world over.

My co-stars, Rainer Devon and Jordan Wilder, and I are more than movie stars now. We're celebrities. We have the number-one film. *Locked*. August, Noah and Ed – the characters we play – are household names. Our love triangle has captivated the world. 100 million book sales. 250 million at the box office opening weekend. Action figures. Our faces are plastered everywhere. Billboards on Sunset Blvd. The cover of every weekly.

Locked*'s Stars Are Rising*

All The RAIGE: Paige and Rainer, love at last

Rainer Devon: Paige is the Reason this Series Works

Jordan Wilder and Rainer Devon Repair Their Relationship

Raige Plays House

We've been on an international press tour for the last four weeks to promote our movie. Paris, Hong Kong, Singapore, Rome, London. A different city every night, sometimes every four hours. I've woken up more often lately not knowing where I am than having a clue.

But now I know. Now we're home. Or at least, L.A.

"How are you doing?" Rainer's voice comes warm in my ear, and I let my body lean against his as we make our way off of this, our last flight.

"Good," I say. "I'm glad we're here." Tour was pretty incredible. All those screaming fans, all that energy. But I'm ready for some down time. I don't think I've slept through the night since we walked down the red carpet at the L.A. premiere.

Rainer pulls me tighter to him. It will be our last embrace until we get in our car. Tawny, our publicist and media coach, has strict rules about that—no touching when there are cameras. No touching outside because there could be cameras. Keep your hands to yourself. Sometimes I feel like I'm back in preschool.

Personally, I think it drives the mania. Hiding, I mean. People know we're together—I did announce it a press conference, after all—but they are so desperate for footage of us hand in hand they're on the hunt for it constantly. Rainer is super active on social media. He's always trying to get me to tweet. He showed me how it works while we were in Rome. He gets thousands of tweets a minute, most of them asking about what it's like to be us. I don't know how I'd possibly answer that, let alone in 140 characters.

Because what is it like to be us? How can I possibly explain the dream come true it is to be a movie star. To be with Rainer. I get to live out two fantasies simultaneously. I get to be August, Noah's lover, and Paige, Rainer's girlfriend. And I'm grateful for that. But it's also only half of it. It doesn't include the parts I don't know how to talk about, things I can't mention in interviews. That I feel like I'm inside a blender. I can't tell my toes from my brain. There are times when I wonder where August ends and Paige begins, and that scares me. It scares me more than the flashbulbs and paparazzi. It scares me to think I may not know who I am anymore.

All I know is that I'm with Rainer, and Rainer can handle this. Fame, fantasy, everything in the middle. He's not only okay in the spotlight, he thrives in it. And that's who I need by my side right now—someone who can stand with me. Even if he's not holding my hand.

As much as I'd like to walk out of the airport next to him, I'm also not desperate for photos of us making out to land at the grocery store my parents go to, either. So I'll stick with Tawny's frenzy-inducing rules.

We make our way downstairs and at the top of the escalator, Rainer lets me go. He'll move a few stairs down so it won't be possible to get a photo of us together. I know the drill.

"The car will be waiting. Three minutes," he tells me. "It's never more than three minutes." He says the same thing to me in every city. It's his mantra. Ours.

I nod. I kiss him. Once, on the lips.

"See you on the flip side."

Our bodyguards appear, out of nowhere, and then we're down in baggage claim. I step off the escalator.

I don't know how they know when we're going to land. Especially this early in the morning. Does someone tip them off? Are our travel schedules somehow public? Do they spend every day here waiting for celebrities to get off flights? I tuck my head down. I keep my eyes trained on the feet in front of me. One. Two. Three.

I hear them before I see them. They scream: Paige! My name, like a shotgun.

I see Rainer outside the glass double-doors. He swings his backpack into the waiting black Escalade and I empty out my lungs.

"Paige! Is it true that you and Rainer are engaged?" "Paige! How is Rainer handling the scandal with Britney Drake and his father?" "Paige! Where is Jordan Wilder?"

Don't react. That's what they tell you. They tell you to keep a positive face, to smile. To never let them see you sweat. But none of that helps with the giant, unquestionable need I have to tell them the truth. To set the record straight.

No, we're not engaged. We haven't even talked about next week, let alone the rest of our lives.

Not well. Rainer is not handling the fact that his father tried to sleep with his ex girlfriend well. Thanks for asking!

And lastly: I have no idea where Jordan Wilder is.

Jordan, the third point of our infamous *Locked* love triangle, left London a week ago with Alexis Gibson. Alexis is playing Maggie my—August's—sister. She was on set for maybe two days during the first shoot but she's a major player in the second movie—and she came on the last half of the press tour with us.

According to Rainer, Jordan's always had a thing for Alexis—the one girl he's "been trying to land forever."

Not that it's my business. Not anymore.

"Paige! Will you and Rainer be living together?"

Nate, one of our security guys, holds the Escalade door

open for me and then I'm inside. Rainer is there, but he doesn't immediately reach for me. The paparazzi are still shooting through the windshield—the only window in the car that isn't fully tinted.

One more question—something I can't hear but that I see makes Rainer sink, makes him cringe—and then we're driving away.

"Not so bad," Rainer says the second we're out of sight. I reach for him at the same moment he pulls me in. His hands go around my waist then up to my shoulders and then he cups both my cheeks with his hands.

"Hey," he says. He leans down close and kisses me—his mouth presses hard over mine. My hands move up to his neck and then thread through his hair.

"Not so bad," I say. He pulls me even tighter. "I need a shower. I'm gross."

He lets his mouth rest on my ear. When he talks I feel his breath there—warm and charged—like it carries an electric current. "Beg to differ."

I roll my eyes but his arms stay around me and I don't try to wriggle away. Every day with Rainer, every moment going through this insane tornado of insta-fame, makes me more certain that I made the right decision. Rainer can be there in a way I really need. Rainer is home in all of this. And Jordan . . .

What is there to say about Jordan that even matters

anymore? Jordan has no ability to deal with fame. He's more uncomfortable with his own celebrity than I am with mine. We did one event together without Rainer. It was a *Locked* book launch on Maui, and Jordan completely deserted me in the crowds. If we were together, we'd probably be in a bunker somewhere, hiding out. And I haven't read all the fine print of my contract, but I'm pretty sure that's not allowed.

The second the premiere ended, and I chose Rainer, Jordan and I became something close to strangers. He would barely talk to me on the press tour and before Alexis joined us, he brought a different girl back to the hotel every night.

My best friend, Cassandra, says he's acting out, that he's trying to prove something, but I don't know. It's like he doesn't even care, like he's forgotten those moments we shared on Maui. I guess it's better if he forgets. We both should.

The one saving grace in all of this is that Rainer and Jordan are being civil. I know how painful it was when Rainer thought Britney and Jordan had cheated on him, before he learned the truth about his father. They're not besties or anything, but Rainer no longer wants to punch Jordan every time he sees him. That's progress.

"Should we stop off for breakfast?" Rainer asks me. "It is a special day."

I raise an eyebrow at him. "Rainer. Shower. Imperative."

He lets his eyes flit downward, just slightly, but it's enough to make me blush. "Home it is."

Sandy rented me an apartment in Beverly Hills "fit for Hollywood's latest It Girl," but I couldn't bring myself to stay there alone. It was just too big and empty. So unbeknownst to my parents, I was crashing at Rainer's before we left town. He had rented a place in Bel Air, off Stone Canyon, when everything went down with his dad at the premiere and he needed to move out of his parents'— fast.

We stayed at the Bel Air house for two weeks before we left on tour. I loved it. It's peaceful and quiet and *secluded*, which right now feels like more of a luxury than private jets, Monaco, and uninterrupted sleep combined. I have no plans to leave anytime soon.

I can feel my body relax as the driver types in the code and the electric gate peels back revealing the house—all glass windows—surrounded by trees.

"I'll deal with the bags," Rainer says. "Go ahead."

I thank the driver and walk up the path. The door gives easily. I slide my backpack down in the entrance, take off my shoes, and let my toes feel the hard wood underneath my feet. Home. Or as close to it as I have right now.

My cell rings as soon as I'm inside. I hit answer. "I'm back," I say. "Just landed."

I hear my mom's voice bright and clear through the phone. "Everyone, Paige is back!" Some half-hearted mumbling and screeching on the part of my niece, Annabelle. I feel a slight tug at my chest. I miss her. She's growing so fast and I can't help but feel kind of guilty that I'm not there to see it, and to help out with her. When my sister, Joanna, got pregnant, in high school, raising Annabelle became a team effort. "How was the flight?"

"Long," I say. "Glad to be back. I got you those postcards you wanted from Paris."

"Oh, perfect," she says. "And did you get that ribbon for your sister? She wants all the bridesmaids to wear it in their hair."

"Got it, Mom." My sister's wedding is still a while away. I'm the maid of honor—a role I was born to play, I guess? Although since I'm not there, most of the role-duties have fallen to my mom.

"Honey, I was just telling your father I think this is the first year we're not together . . ."

I see Rainer stumble through the front door, carrying three different duffle bags. "Mom, I gotta go. Rainer is about to throw out his back."

"Have a great day!" she says. "We love you."

"Love you too," I say, hanging up.

I go over to Rainer and loop one of the bags onto my shoulder. "Show off," I tell him.

"Anything to impress you." He kisses me once on the lips and I plod down the hallway to the master bedroom, feeling happy.

Before the premiere it was total chaos but tour was different. Despite the crazy call times and barely-there sleep schedule we had all of this time to just be together. For real this time, with no secrets. When I chose Rainer at the premiere, with all those journalists there, I solidified our fate together. And we've just been getting closer every day since. My face gets hot thinking about our recent hotel-room stints.

I close the door and peel my clothes off as I make my way into the bathroom. It's giant, bigger than my entire kitchen back home, and all of it marble. It has two shower heads. You could spend half an hour in here and never fog up the sink windows—they're that far away.

I step in, letting the water pour down over my head and wash away the flight, the airport, the last month. It feels so good. I exhale out everything I've been holding.

As I start lathering up my hair I think about today. No schedules, no interviews. Free zone to do whatever I want. We can order pizza. I can let my hair air dry! That one thought alone makes me giggle in the shower.

I finish up, flip a towel around my head and slip on a fluffy white bathrobe—a gift from Rainer. It's even monogrammed with his nickname for me: *PG*. Every fan wants to know what he's like as a boyfriend and here's the truth: he's just as great as you think he is. There are plenty of things I have to lie about. My sleep schedule (I like to get eight hours!), my beauty regimen (masks and moisturizer!), my diet (no cheeseburgers!) but I've never had to lie about how wonderful Rainer is. The world is right—when I'm in a blender, he's the off button. I'm crazy lucky.

"Rainer?"

My wet feet make smacking sounds on the wood floor. The house is strangely quiet. "Rainer?"

I see him sitting on the couch in the middle of the giant living room. There isn't much furniture in this house, just the basics. I love that about it here. There is so much excess everywhere else in our lives right now it's nice to come home somewhere that is just essential, just what we need.

I see him hunched over the coffee table. I start walking to him but before I can ask what's going on I see the stack of mail in front of him—everything we've missed while we were gone. Newspapers, magazines. I let my palms move over them, spreading them slightly. They've all splashed versions of the same headline across the cover page: *Greg Devon, studio executive, dethroned.*

Greg Devon denies sexual harassment allegations.

Devon—Hollywood's Devil.

On, and on, and on.

I sink down onto the couch next to Rainer. I put my

arms around him. The towel falls and my wet hair tumbles down onto his face. I push it back. I pick his face up to look into mine. "I'm here," I tell him softly. "We're in this together." I can't imagine what it must be like for him—to have his family shamed so publicly. I know he hates his father, as he should, but I also know it's not easy to see a man he loved, and respected, be ground to a pulp—even if he deserves it.

Rainer slips his hand into mine. He squeezes. "I know," he says. "And thank you. But I don't want to get into this now." He pushes the papers away. "I'm not ruining today." He cups my chin in his hand and then he's kissing me, gently at first, and then stronger.

"You want coffee?" he asks me, a little bit breathless.

"Definitely."

He gets up from the couch. He's wearing a T-shirt and grey sweats. His hair is still rumpled from the plane. God, he's cute.

"Stop staring," he says, smiling. "We have a lot to do today."

"I don't want to *do* anything today," I say. "I just want to hang out here with you."

He raises an eyebrow before he disappears into the kitchen. "Listen, if what you really want for your birthday is to take advantage of me, I'm not going to argue with you."

"What?"

He pokes his head out from behind the wall. His dimples are dancing. "Your *birthday*, PG. Otherwise known as the day I get to stop feeling like such a cradle-robbing old man. You better get on US time quick."

April 5th. Eighteen.

"I totally forgot."

"Well lucky for you, your boyfriend didn't." Rainer comes back and sets a steaming mug down on the coffee table. Before I can form another thought, his lips brush mine. With his free hand he traces his fingers down my shoulders, wraps them around my back and pulls me closer. My hands flutter to his shoulders. I pull him in.

"You know if I took a picture right now I could sell it and retire." I break away from Rainer and see Sandy standing in the doorway, her arms crossed, a horizontal smirk on her face. "Welcome back, guys," she says. "We need to talk."

CHAPTER 2

Sandy comes towards us, a whirlwind of cream and silk in the form of a slim, blonde, forty-something woman. She surveys us, her hands on her lips. "Happy Birthday, PG," she says.

Sandy is Rainer's manager and now mine, too. I hired her before we left for tour but she's been my acting manager practically since I got the role of August in *Locked*—and more than that, she's been a mentor and friend. She's basically acting mom to all of us.

"Thanks."

"Before you guys make any plans, we have to talk about those offers that are rolling in for the two of you." She looks at me and says, "Sorry, kid, the machine rests for no birthday. You're lucky I didn't show up at the airport." She cocks her head at Rainer. "How do you feel about being a young Superman?"

He gasps. So do I. "Are you serious?"

"Dead. And you—" Sandy loops her finger in the air. "Have you read any of the scripts I gave you?"

"A few," I say. She sent twenty: romantic comedies, a few high school dramas, and one totally amazing script called *Closer to Heaven* about a girl who leaves home at sixteen to join the circus and ends up becoming the greatest high wire artist in the world. It's one of the most beautiful scripts I've ever read and that's saying a lot—there was a time in my life where I read ten a week, easy.

"*Closer to Heaven*," I say. "I want to talk to the writer."

Sandy bites her bottom lip. "I was afraid you'd say that. They got Billy Zack to direct and he thinks you're too blockbuster."

"That's insane," Rainer says. "Why are you sending Paige twenty scripts? I only ever get three."

"Because I know what you like. Anyway, Paige, you'd be better off doing something else. That one will pay nothing."

"I don't care," I say. "It was the only one I read that I loved."

"Listen," Rainer says, reaching over and kneading one of my shoulders. "I think this is a conversation for another time. We just got home. It's Paige's birthday."

Sandy nods. "But I need you to move forward with something soon," she says, pointing her finger at me. "And I came all the way up the canyon to impress this upon you in person."

"Hey, have you heard from Wyatt?" Rainer asks. We

read online that Wyatt wasn't directing the next movie, which I guess would explain why he left the tour after the first week. He was tough, but we loved him, and it feels weird to be moving on to the next movie without him. "He isn't returning our calls."

"He's doing another movie," she says. She looks resigned. "*I* haven't even heard from Wyatt. But we need to get comfortable with the reality that he's not going to be with us on the next film." She runs a hand over her forehead and I know there is more at work here than just business. I always suspected Wyatt and Sandy had a complicated "friendship."

Rainer exhales. "We just want to talk to him."

It's almost odd seeing Rainer this attached to Wyatt—after all they clashed for most of the movie. But by the end Wyatt became like a dad to us. I know Rainer can't imagine losing him now, too.

Sandy flips her wrist to look at her watch. "Alright, moving on. Your father called."

"Not this again," Rainer says.

Sandy sticks her hands on her hips. "Look, you don't want him to be your father? Cool. I don't think anyone could blame you. But he's still your producer."

Rainer turns around and crosses his arms. "What's that supposed to mean?"

Sandy gives her best *come on* expression. "What do you think it means?" she says. She's playing hardball with him, and he knows it. I see him hiccup back a laugh.

"You think I care?" he says.

Sandy shrugs. "About being replaced in this franchise? Yeah, I kinda do."

Does Greg Devon have that kind of power? Of course he does. He hired us all; there's no reason he couldn't fire us.

"Hey, Rainer, can I see you for a minute?" I say.

Rainer follows me into the bedroom. When we're alone together, I feel the quiet of the room palpably. It's like there is someone else in here that is taking up all the space, all the air. He goes over to the window.

"She's right, you know," I say.

Rainer doesn't respond.

I move up closer to him and put my hand on his back. He flinches, but he doesn't move away from my touch. "Maybe you should talk to him."

"How can I?" he asks. His voice is quiet. I realize: he's not angry, he's sad.

"He's your father," I say. "No matter what else has happened that's still true."

He turns around to me and I see that his face is hard, set. He's so much paler now that he's not playing Noah. He looks almost ghostlike compared to how he was on the island. "He tried to sleep with my nineteen-year-old girlfriend," he says. "How do I forgive that?"

"I don't know," I say, truthfully. "Maybe you don't.

But you can't cut your family out forever."

Rainer's eyes are cold. "Why not?"

"Because you heard Sandy: he's our producer, too. He's going to be in our lives." I hug my arms around me. I want to reach out and touch him, but I'm not sure how I would be received.

"Maybe, maybe not." Rainer shakes his head, turning back to the window.

"You know we don't have a choice. If they want us for the next movie—and it's pretty clear they do—we have to do the next movie."

Rainer doesn't turn. "It's humiliating. The thought of being a part of something he created, that he made happen? I hate it. And now Wyatt might not even be on board. Who knows what kind of shitty sequel this could be?"

"Well, I'll be in it. And so far my track record is pretty good." I'm trying to lighten the mood, but a part of me worries that Rainer could find a way out of it. How could I even think of doing these movies without him? It's us—on camera and off. I need him next to me in all my worlds.

Rainer sighs as he starts towards me, his feet padding across the hard wood floor. In another moment, his hands are on my shoulders and he is staring right at me.

"I'm sorry," he says. He puts his hands on either side of my face and then he's drawing me towards him. His lips meet mine and his hands move down my back. They feel solid there, strong, and I let myself go pliant against his chest, the tension of the last minutes flowing out of me. "I don't mean for this to involve us." He pulls back and touches his forehead to mine.

A knock on the door makes us lift our heads up, but Rainer keeps his arms around me.

"Yeah?" he says.

Sandy comes into view. "I'm heading out, but don't forget the awards next week. The stylist is coming by tomorrow with some dress options for you."

The MTV Movie Awards. I'm nominated for Best Female Performance and Best Kiss . . . twice—once with Rainer and once with Jordan. My first awards show, and there's absolutely no chance Rainer and I are *not* going to win Best Kiss. As proud as I am to stand beside him on the carpet I don't love the idea of having to kiss him onstage in front of all those people. Especially since I know Jordan will be watching us, sitting right in the front row.

"You look like I just sacrificed a puppy," Sandy says. "It's an awards show—you dress up, you get your picture taken, you watch some people sing and dance and say things they'll probably regret the next day . . . It's fun. Speaking of which, have some fun today. Just don't get photographed with a champagne bottle between your knees."

"That's specific."

"You'd be surprised," Sandy says, waving goodbye.

CHAPTER 3

"Wow," Rainer says. He's leaning against the bedroom door, dressed in jeans, a button down, and a navy blazer. My breath catches a little when I look at him. He is so damn handsome. "You look incredible."

I glance down at my black slip-dress—something Tawny got me for press tour that I kept, because it was one of the only things I actually liked. It's not as binding as everything else they had me in. Tawny said it was sexy, but understated—which fits the bill for tonight.

I have my hair up in a loose ponytail and I'm wearing the gold cowry shell necklace Rainer gave me at the end of the shoot. I've even put on some makeup—I learned a thing or two from hours in the chair with Lillianna, our makeup director on the first movie. "Thanks."

"Come here."

He takes my hand and leads me over to the bed. "Rainer . . ."

"I just want to give you your present."

I look at him, his dimples winking. The box is blue velvet, and small. The size of a ring. I feel my heart begin to pound in my throat. He wouldn't. I know he wouldn't. I don't care how many tabloid stories about his proposal there have been. We haven't been really, truly together that long, and I'm only eighteen; he wouldn't ask me to marry him. Would he?

He shifts on the bed and I feel my pulse in my ears. He's twenty-two. In Hollywood that's close to forty.

"It'd be nice to give it to you on your actual birthday," Rainer says, nodding towards the box. "Any day now you can open it."

I take a deep breath. My hands shake as they pop up the lid. Inside is a ring, but it's not an engagement ring. It's a gold cowry shell, just like my necklace, except this one is encrusted with tiny diamonds.

I exhale all the air I've been holding. I reach up and put a hand through his hair. "I love it," I say.

Rainer covers my fingers with his own. "Good." He leans down and kisses me, but it's brief. "Here," he says. He slips the ring out of its case and onto my middle finger.

"Perfect fit," I say.

"Like us."

I make a face and he laughs. "This is why I don't write my own dialogue," he says. "Come on, your party awaits."

"Party?"

"PG," he says, running a thumb over my cheek. "It's your eighteenth. You didn't really think you'd escape without a party."

"Please tell me you didn't," I say.

Rainer plants a quick kiss on my cheek. "Unfortunately, babe, I did."

We have some champagne in the limo, and by the time we pull up to the restaurant the bubbles are creating a hazy, sunset-y feel in my stomach. My head is light and airy, and I slip my hand into Rainer's as we step out into the night.

They've shut down the back of Via Alloro, an Italian restaurant in Beverly Hills that Rainer loves. I feel giddy that I'm getting to see some of his L.A. life on my birthday.

The back of the restaurant is all open air and it's a gorgeous night. They have heat lamps going and the trees are lit up with tiny twinkle lights. There are delicious things everywhere—trays of champagne and miniature appetizers. And I see a giant cake sitting on a table—spiraled letters spelling out "Happy Birthday, PG."

"You're way too much," I tell Rainer.

"Just wait." He takes my hand and winds me to a table

in the very back of the space where people are gathered. But not just any people. *My* people. Cassandra and Jake.

"Happy Birthday!" Cassandra says, launching herself into my arms. I hold her tight, breathing in the familiar smell of my best friend.

"Happy bday," Jake says. He tries to go in for a hug but is instantly squashed by Cassandra, who still won't let go.

"Sorry I didn't call," Cassandra says, pulling back briefly. "I was on a plane."

She grins at me. She has on a floral print dress, leggings, and giant red sunglasses that keep sliding down her nose. I look at Rainer who is smiling, his arms folded across his chest. "Told you," he says. "I give the best gifts."

I toss him an OMG glance and then I yelp and squeeze Cassandra close again. "You're here!" I say, still not believing it.

"Duh."

I pull back and hold her at arm's length. She smiles wide and my heart feels like it's going to burst.

"Glad to see I've flown all this way to come in a clear second." Jake knocks my shoulder and then he's opening his arms wide and hugging both of us.

"C'mon," Cassandra says into his chest. "Like it was going to be another way."

Jake shrugs, releasing us. "I'll take it. Hey, you look

great." He says it offhand and for the briefest of moments I remember Jake and I kissing in my living room. But it's such a distant memory it feels as if it belongs to someone else.

I put my hands on his shoulders. "Thanks for coming," I say.

He wraps his arms around me and even though Cassandra and Rainer are right next to us I pull him in tighter. He's family. In some ways even more than my own. Joanna and my parents came out for the premiere, but I haven't seen my brothers since the last time I was home.

"You may suffocate him," Cassandra says when I finally let Jake go. I glance over at her, but she's smiling, unconcerned. "He'd probably let you. He's experiencing so much guilt about that *plane ride*." She mouths the last two words to me.

"My carbon footprint was impeccable until you became a movie star," he says.

"Sorry about that."

I feel Rainer slip a hand around my waist. "You mean you didn't at all enjoy those reclining seats? The candy?" he says. "Sour patch kids are your guilty pleasure, right?"

I turn my head to him. "Candy?"

Rainer shrugs. "I had them stock the plane."

"You flew them private?"

Rainer smiles and cups my chin with his hand. "They're

your best friends." I let his lips graze mine. "Plus it was the clear way to guilt Jake into it. I donated the carbon offset."

Jake slings an arm over Cassandra's. "Your parents send their regrets, by the way," he says.

"They're deep in wedding planning," Cassandra continues. "And Joanna couldn't find anyone to watch Annabelle."

"We tried," Rainer says.

"You guys being here is everything." I glance back at the table and wave to Jessica, Wyatt's assistant, and Alexis—who is, apparently, attending my birthday party.

I peel myself away from Rainer and loop my arm through Cassandra's. "I need to borrow you," I say.

"No borrowing necessary. I'm yours."

Jake clears his throat. "For a limited period of time. Also I want to talk to you about how you can use this newfound celebrity for good." His face gets super serious. "You have an amazing platform now, but all I see printed about you are dating gossip columns about how this dude kisses," he says, gesturing to Rainer.

I'm remembering this piece that ran before tour about how Rainer had rented out a movie theater for a romantic date we had. It was true. I still don't know how they found out about it. Someone Rainer had let in to plan it? Reading it was strange. It was like the reporter had been to a different version of our night. We had popcorn, not

Skittles. We did make out, though. This is what I'm saying: being famous is like being yourself, but not. It's like being yourself outside of yourself. There are two versions—the one you know and the one people think they know and it's hard to remember which is which. It's easy to start believing what people write about you.

"I brought a lot of introductory materials," Jake says.

I glance at Rainer and he nods. "Jake and I will get started on saving the world. You two do . . .whatever girls do."

I lead Cassandra away from the table into a corner by a lightly radiating heat lamp. As soon as we're alone, Cassandra corners me. "How is it going with Rainer? Tell me *everything*."

"Things are really good," I say. "He was amazing on tour. Cassandra, you would have not believed how crazy it was."

Cassandra nods. "I saw pics."

"It was bigger than anything you can imagine."

"Scary," Cassandra says.

"I know. But Rainer is great with it all. Seriously, Cass, I don't know what I'd do without him. He's so supportive—"

"And hot," Cassandra says. She clucks her tongue and raises her eyebrows. I look over at where Rainer is handing Jake a drink.

"And hot," I agree.

Cassandra takes my hand in hers. "I can't believe it," she says. "You're this movie star." Her blue eyes look into mine. They're bright. Piercing. "I'm really proud of you," she says.

I feel something well up in my throat. I hug her close and she yelps.

"Ask me about Jake," she says.

I laugh. "I'm sorry! How is Jake?"

She sucks in her bottom lip. "Great," she says. "I mean he still makes me stand outside superstores on Saturdays, but I don't even mind anymore. It's fun when we're together. Can you believe it?"

"Yeah," I say. "I sorta can. You two look really happy."

"I am . . ." Her gaze drifts over to him. "I think he's making me a better person. Isn't that gross?"

"No," I say. "That's amazing."

She wrinkles her nose. "Who would have thought we'd both fall in love *for* the first time *at* the same time."

Love.

"So," Cassandra says. She squints at me. "You think Jordan will show tonight?"

I glance at Alexis. "No idea. You think Rainer would invite him?"

Cassandra shrugs. "You said they're being civil again, right? Maybe as a gesture?"

I finally confessed to Cassandra that something had gone on with Jordan and I on Maui. I told her after the premiere. Well actually, she guessed it. We were with my sister, but she had stepped out to call her fiancé, Bill, when Cassandra sprung the question on me. I told her the truth: that I had feelings for Jordan but that I had made a choice, and I was happy with it.

"Yeah," I say. "Maybe."

"Have you spoken to him since you've been back?"

"Since this morning? No. He's . . ." I let my voice trail off. I don't know how to finish that sentence. What *is* Jordan? Angry? Missing in action? Definitely over me.

I think about Jordan at the press conference. How he looked at me with so much understanding and compassion. Love, maybe, even. But on tour all of that was gone. He treated me like a leper. Wherever I was, he definitely was not.

I drop my voice even lower. "He seemed pretty cozy with Alexis on tour."

Cassandra raises an eyebrow at me. "No chance."

"You've seen her, right?" I say, cocking my head in the direction of the table. "Plus, apparently he's always had some thing for her."

"Well maybe that's good," she says. "You're with Rainer, right?"

"Yeah," I say. "Of course."

Just then Jake and Rainer come over. "Sorry to interrupt," Rainer says. "But you *are* the guest of honor."

"Who, me?" Cassandra says, blinking at him. I know she means to wink, but she's never been able to do it. "Fine, I'll go greet my adoring fans."

The four of us head over the table. Alexis immediately stands. "Happy Birthday," she says in her perfect British accent. "I've missed you, darling."

I try to keep my eyes on her, to stop them from darting around the space, trying to see if he's here.

"Alexis," I say. "How are you?"

Alexis is dressed, as usual, effortlessly cooly. Jeans, heels, a silk shirt, and a color-contrasting head scarf. Gold and turquoise jewelry hangs from her neck and ears. She's tall, too—about 5'9 to my 5'2. She used to be a model—the real kind. Fashion. She grew up all over the world—Paris, London, Portugal. I can't hate her, though, because she's genuinely trying to be my friend. I can't even resent Jordan for wanting her—who wouldn't?

I suddenly feel really, really short in my black dress. I normally like being short, but it may not have killed me to wear heels tonight instead of these low wedges.

"Wonderful. How are you? Not jet-lagged, I hope?"

"Not too bad," I say, accepting champagne from a passing waiter. "We slept a lot on the plane."

I wave at Jessica and she cranes over the table to give

me a hug before I feel Alexis grabbing at me. "Let me see this!" she says.

She snatches my hand up from my side and gapes at the ring Rainer just gave me.

I snuggle closer into him. "It goes with my necklace." I pluck it off my chest.

"Gorgeous," she says. "Rainer has impeccable taste." And then her voice changes. She gestures behind me. "Wilder," Alexis says over my shoulder. "You're late."

Instantly, I look up, and the second I do, I see him.

He's coming down the path to the table. He's backlit by hanging Chinese lanterns, and I'm reminded of the first time I saw him, on the beach in Hawaii, framed by the sun. That was back when I thought he was an asshole, when I was convinced he was out to ruin Rainer's life, and by association, mine. Before I got to know him. Before I understood everything he had lost and everything he still wanted.

"Happy Birthday." He looks at me for a beat and I swear, my heart stops. I'm sure Rainer can feel the blood rushing through my body from where his hand still sits perched on my hip. I feel Jordan's eyes drift over me. They feel like fingers, like they're weighted, somehow.

"Thanks," I mumble. The most we've said to each other in weeks.

His so-brown-it's-black hair sits ruffled on his head and

he has on jeans and a grey blazer over a blue T-shirt. He gives Alexis a quick kiss on the cheek and I look away.

They're together. You have a boyfriend. You're not allowed to feel this way anymore, I remind myself. I swing into action.

"Hey, Alexis, Jordan—these are my best friends Cassandra and Jake. Guys, this is Jordan and this—" I gesture to the gazelle standing next to me— "Is Alexis."

Cassandra eyes Jordan way too obviously, and I see him look back at her. "We met briefly when you guys were out here for the premiere," he says.

"It was just for a second before the screening," Cassandra says. "It's good to see you."

"You too," Jordan says.

"How lovely," Alexis says, taking Jordan's arm. "We're all together."

I kind of hate her.

The table is round, and she and Jordan sit, Jake and Cassandra following suit with Jessica behind them. Rainer does too and Alexis taps the seat next to her, so I'm in between her and Rainer. I'm just grateful I'm not seated next to Jordan. Being in between the two of them takes all the acting I can muster, and tonight, I'm not sure I have it in me.

"Do you have to file environmental impact reports?" Jake is asking.

I hear Alexis in my ear. "So, what is the birthday girl drinking?"

Alexis and I haven't really gotten a chance to know each other. We were a split group on tour—me and Rainer, Jordan and Alexis.

But here, at dinner, we embark on a marathon get-acquainted session. I find out that not only did Alexis grow up in and around Europe but that her mother also lives in Los Angeles, her father has a summer home in the south of France, and she attended boarding school for "one horrid year" in Switzerland. Also fun: she speaks four languages and has two albums out. But none of that compares to the way Jordan watches her—transfixed—like she's some kind of transcendent creature.

"Happy?" Rainer whispers into my ear as I twirl some spaghetti onto my fork.

I blink and look at him. His lashes are so long and with his face this close to me I can almost feel them. My skin instantly pricks up with goosebumps. "Mhm," I whisper. "Thank you. Tonight is perfect."

I feel his hand on my neck. "It's not over," he whispers.

I pull back and look at him and my face must reveal some kind of surprise because he laughs—a soft, twinkling laugh— "we're just going out after dinner," he says. "If you want to?"

"Yeah," I say. "I want to."

Rainer turns his attention to the table. He taps his knife against his glass and everyone hushes. "I'd like to make a toast," he says.

My stomach starts fluttering. I catch Cassandra's eye across the table and she winks at me—but it comes out as a blink—a quirk of hers.

"Happy Birthday, PG." He looks at me and I feel his hand graze mine underneath the table. I thread our fingers together. I need something to hold on to. "I'm so goddamn lucky you were born today. Thank you for trying out for this movie and for being my August." He raises his glass up and then he kisses me. I lean into him and taste the champagne on his mouth and even though I know everyone is watching—Alexis and Jessica and Cassandra and Jake and Jordan, I tell myself not to care. He's my boyfriend. He's kissing me on my birthday. This is the life I chose. All I'm doing is living it.

We go to a club close by or it could be far away—I'm not sure. All I know is that I'm caught up in the night—in the limo that appears out of nowhere, in the champagne, in Rainer's cool fingers on my thigh, just above my knee.

The club is dark when we enter. Jordan is fastened to Alexis's side and she air kisses a group of girls as soon as we get in and pulls Jordan with her—over to a booth. I see him glance back at us, briefly, but then he's lost in the darkness.

I would have had a hard time keeping track of Cassandra and Jake, but Sandy dropped them back off at the house. They claimed exhaustion, but I know dancing isn't really Jake's thing. I also suspect they're excited to spend an unsupervised night alone together. Cassandra's parents are pretty strict.

"Enjoy it," Cassandra says into my ear as she goes, and I just smile because I know what she means. Tonight, on my birthday, we can just be Rainer and Paige. We're not at a press event. We're not on a carpet. We're just *us*. And if being us means we get into private parties at clubs—then so be it.

I feel Rainer's hand on my wrist and then his fingers at my hip as he's moving me towards the dance floor. The music blares around us—a techno version of some pop song I have been hearing on the radio constantly. It's so loud it vibrates through me—like my muscle fibers are a sound system—inputting every beat.

The crowd doesn't seem to notice us as we move through the pulsing bodies. I feel anonymous in this mass and it's delicious, heady, like I could be anyone and do anything. By the time we get to the center of the dance floor I've forgotten we're famous.

I pull Rainer close and loop my arms around his neck.

He drops his lips down until they hover over mine. I dig my fingers into his shoulders. I feel the muscles there move as he presses his hands flat against my back and draws me in closer.

My heart is hammering—trying to keep up with the music and his hands as they trace over me like stencils, creating patterns and shapes in their wake.

I can hear Rainer's breath in my ear and his hand finds mine. He makes an impatient sound and then he's dragging me back out the way we came. I don't bother to look back—to see where Jordan is—whether he's found Alexis in that dark mass the way Rainer has found me. It doesn't matter.

The paparazzi have evidently found all of us because when we leave, there is a sea of photographers—so many flashes it feels like daylight. Rainer tucks me to his side and two bodyguards usher us into a waiting town car. I bury my face in Rainer's shoulder and let his arms circle around me.

"Drive," I hear him say. His tone is tense, frayed around the edges with what we've taken with us from that dance floor.

We speed away but I keep myself fastened to Rainer's side. We find each other in the back of that town car the way we did in the dark club. I'm so caught up in Rainer, in what it feels like to be this close to him that I'm barely aware of coming home and Rainer carrying me through the door.

When we get into the bedroom, he hesitates. We've slept in the same bed before—here, and on tour—but never exactly like this. Never with the air crackling between us like it's something live—something with a heartbeat and pulse all its own.

"It's okay," I say.

His eyes float over me—like the blue in them has turned from ice to water. It swims around his pupils—liquid velvet. He lays me down on the bed. "I'm so glad we're here," he says. He reaches up and tucks my hair behind my ear and then we're kissing and he's pulling me up to him. My fingers find the edge of his shirt and I'm inching it up his torso and then taking it off. I see his chest—his golden muscles working. I've seen him without a shirt on so many times before—countless shoots, the beach, for months, and the familiarity of it—of the little indent he has on the right side of his ribcage and the birthmark right above his belly button—fills me with a joy I can't quite describe. I know him, now, and he knows me—in a way no one else does or ever will. Because he's in this with me. It's just the two of us. And it's this that makes me kiss him back harder, fiercer.

His hands are in my hair and then they slide down my body. I feel his fingers on my waist, then down to my hips and I arch up against his lips. He moves to the zipper on my dress and I all of a sudden realize I don't have a bra on underneath. I didn't wear one because the straps showed.

The realization makes me edge back, just a tiny bit, but it's enough for Rainer's hands to stop what they're doing.

"Are you okay?" he asks me. His voice is ragged and I can feel his heartbeat through his skin—as haphazard as my own.

I nod, except I'm not sure. If my dress is opened then so is this whole new dimension and all of a sudden I don't know if I'm ready for that. It's like I'm seeing myself outside of myself—watching me. The way everyone else is. And I don't want them to see this. I don't want them to know. Suddenly something Jessica showed me months ago on set comes flashing back to me—she read me some fan-fiction about me and Rainer. Not August and Noah, me and Rainer. It was meant to be a little bit silly, but now it all comes hurling back. The paragraphs of us together, just like this. The remembered sentences come one after the other— they pile on top of my chest until I can feel their weight physically. It's like we're in somebody else's fantasy. I thought we were alone tonight, but we're not. The whole universe is in bed with us.

"What is it?" Rainer asks. I can see the concern in his eyes and it lessens the pressure, just a little. "What's wrong?" His palm finds my cheek and he holds it there. "Talk to me."

But I don't know what to say. How can I explain that being with him right now, like this, feels like we're fulfilling some public wish? Like we're in somebody else's fantasy?

"I'm scared," I say, because it's true.

"Of me?"

I shake my head. I can feel my face get hot, am sure his hand on my cheek feels it, too. My eyes fill with tears and I bite my lip to keep them from spilling over. I feel so stupid in this bed with him, so small—I don't know why I can't just be here. Turn my brain off and stop thinking.

"Hey," he says. "It's okay." He moves his hand from my cheek to my temple and rubs his thumb back and forth there. "We have plenty of time. There is no rush here."

"I know," I whisper.

"Good," he says. He slides us down so we're lying against the pillows. He tucks an arm around me and holds my hand against his chest. "Just relax," he says. "Get some sleep." He threads a hand through my hair and I feel his heartbeat slow along with mine.

CHAPTER 4

The next morning we go to breakfast at the Beverly Glenn. The Beverly Glenn is a little shopping center close to the Bel Air house that celebrities often frequent because no one seems to care that you're there. It's hidden up in the hills—just a few boutiques, a restaurant, a salon, and a Starbucks.

Cassandra is chattering about how amazing last night was and Rainer goes to get us all coffees and eggs and muffins and French toast. "I'm glad there are no paps here," Cassandra says. "My hair is having a day."

Jake rolls his eyes at me. I laugh. "What time is your flight?"

"Too soon," Cassandra pouts. She shuffles some papers around in the booth and then squeals. I see a story about us. There is a photo of us from last night leaving the club and my left hand is circled in red. The headline reads: RAINER GIVES PAIGE A PROMISE RING.

I look down at my hand. How do they know he gave me that ring? I make a move to grab for the paper, but Cassandra is already reading. "For her birthday, Rainer gave his beloved Paige or 'PG,' as he affectionately calls her, a promise ring. 'They're too young to get engaged,' a source tells us. 'But Rainer wanted Paige to know he's in it for the long haul. He adores her.'"

Adores her. I grit my teeth. Another private moment made public, and then twisted. A promise ring? I shiver, thinking about last night, about what almost happened but didn't because of this ungranted access.

I grab the paper from Cassandra and toss it into the empty booth behind us. Avoidance is key. "Not before coffee," I say.

"Too young to get engaged, huh?" Cassandra says, swishing her lips at me.

"Stop it," I tell her, kicking her under the table. "This stuff is insane."

"Yeah, but they were right," Cassandra says. "Rainer does adore you."

Jake leans forward. "You okay, PG?"

"Of course," I say, smiling at him. "I'm just letting stupid BS get to me."

Jake shrugs and Rainer comes over with our food. We

eat, but I feel Jake's eyes on me. Something about the way he's looking at me makes me feel like he can see something. Like he knows that in some ways I am decidedly *not* okay. The thing that freaks me out the most, is: If he can see it, who else can?

We have breakfast and then we have to go back to the house and pack them up.

"I wish you were staying," I tell Cassandra. The four of us are outside. The boys are loading luggage into the waiting town car.

"Some of us still have to attend school," she says, her arms around me. "But I'll call you as soon as I land."

"You better."

"You sure you don't want me to drive you?" Rainer asks.

"I'd rather not have a camera in my face while I take off my shoes for security," Jake says.

"What's the deal with not springing for a jet on the way back?" Cassandra says. She pokes Rainer with her elbow. I love watching them interact. I can tell Cassandra really likes him.

"She's demanding," Rainer says to Jake.

"Dude, you have no idea."

Rainer goes to say something to the driver and Jake cocks his head to me. "C'mere," he says.

I follow him a few paces over, so we're out of earshot.

I'm hoping he's not going to ask me any more questions. "Thank you for coming," I say. "It really meant a lot to me."

"We didn't get much time to talk," he says.

"I know. I'm sorry, but your girlfriend is kind of a hog."

He laughs. "I know all of this can't be easy. I just want to tell you that I'm here for you. Whenever you need me, okay, Pat?"

I see his face fall into his droopy grin and then I'm smiling, too. Patrick has always been Jake's nickname for me but I haven't heard him use it since before I left Portland.

He pulls me into a hug. I have to roll up onto my tiptoes to reach.

"You grew," I say.

He laughs. "I guess some things have changed on our end, too."

I watch their car until it has pulled out of the driveway and then head back inside. The phone is ringing.

"You going to get that?" I ask Rainer.

He's in the refrigerator and he pokes his head back to look at me. "I didn't even know we had a home line," he says.

I find the phone on the counter. Some Bang and Olufsen model that has the weight of a penny and an impossible to determine mouthpiece. Which end do you talk into?

"Darling," Alexis says when I answer. Her accent pours through the phone like honey.

"Hey," I say. Is Jordan there? Is he lounging on her couch shirtless as she talks to me?

"Fabulous time last night, please tell Rain."

I glance at him. He's raising his eyebrows at me as if to ask who is it. "Thanks, Alexis. I will."

"I'm calling to see if you want to come to Georgina's."

Georgina is Alexis's best friend. She plays the lead on that hit CW show about aliens. *Elsewhere.* She's dating her co-star, Blake, in real life, but their characters are just secretly in love on the show for now. It's actually kind of addictive. I marathoned all of season 1 on the plane while we were on tour.

"Today?" I glance at Rainer. He smiles encouragingly. "Sure," I say. "Yeah. That works."

"I'll pick you up in an hour," she says. "Bel Air, right? Looking forward to it."

I hang up and look at Rainer. He's coming towards me, an apple in one hand.

"I thought we could spend some time alone this afternoon," I say. "Just the two of us."

"I'd love to," he says. "But I can't. I have to deal with stuff."

"Stuff." I nod. I know he means his dad. "You know you can talk to me about *stuff*," I say.

Rainer takes a bite. "I know. I just want to keep you out of this."

I shake my head. "But I'm not out of this. I'm in this."

"No, you're not. I don't want your name alongside mine in those headlines. It's bad enough I've been dragged into all the stuff with my dad. I'm not dragging you, too." He looks tired, resigned. I notice for the first time that there are circles under his eyes.

"Rainer . . ."

He holds up his hand. "There isn't anything more to say." He reaches out and tucks a strand of hair behind my ear. "Go see the girls. Let me handle this."

Two hours later I'm at Georgina's Malibu Colony beach house. I'm stretched out on a lounge chair, trying to take a nap, but Georgina is chattering to Alexis and me about Blake, her co-star and boyfriend. Apparently she's pissed he's not here with us this weekend.

"He never leaves Atlanta," she tells us, wearily. "He's obsessed with being in character. You're so lucky Rainer is here, Paige."

I make a noncommittal noise.

"Why is my glass empty?" Alexis asks. She's standing above us, clad in a white bikini and giant-brimmed hat. She's blocking my sun.

"Aren't you on a juice cleanse?" Georgina comes over

to Alexis and tops off her glass, spilling some champagne on the floor.

"I think all liquids count," Alexis says, settling herself on the lounge next to me.

Georgina's house is impressive. Alexis told me her money comes from endorsement deals. "Plus her mom created Charlie's Angels or something," Alexis says when Georgina goes inside to get reinforcements.

Speaking of endorsements, I have about twenty offers on the table besides Seven, which I've already partnered with. Burberry, Lancôme, even Chanel. Tawny and Sandy are pushing me for Lancôme—it's the most approachable, they say. And they're trying to reach a younger audience.

I close my eyes, letting the sounds of the ocean lull me. Cassandra isn't here, and I need friends in L.A. This is what Sandy tells me. This is what Rainer tells me. Alexis seems like as good a place as any to start. Besides the small issue that she's probably spending her sleeping hours curled up in some kind of lace negligée with Jordan. I squeeze my eyes tighter, trying to get rid of the image.

"I did not!" Alexis shrieks.

"You didn't what?" I ask.

"You reek of it," Georgina says, ignoring me.

Alexis shakes her head.

"What?" I ask again.

"Hot, all-night-long sex with Jordan Wilder," Georgina says, finishing off her glass.

My stomach plummets.

"I don't kiss and tell," Alexis says. "But if I did, you couldn't handle it." She turns away from us and I have to mentally force myself to unclench my fists at my sides.

Georgina fluffs her bangs. "Well I'm glad to see he's not hung up on Britney anymore."

"He was never hung up on Britney," I say.

Georgina sends Alexis a glance like *what's with her?* "Okay then."

"Have you spoken to Britney?" Alexis asks Georgina.

"Since this Greg stuff? No way. The press is having a field day. Laura would lose her shit if I got within range."

Laura is Georgina's publicist. And from the way she talks about her, her conscience. Georgina only does things of which Laura approves.

"You're such a classy friend," Alexis says.

"You know I'd stand next to you through anything. But Britney never had our backs. I just don't see why we have to have hers."

Alexis doesn't respond, and Georgina hops into the pool and hangs on to the side, kicking her feet out behind her. I want to ask more about Britney, but I don't want to seem over-eager for info or jealous of Rainer's ex, so I keep quiet.

I shrug off my cover up. I'm wearing a bikini I bought in Hawaii—orange with red and gold flowers. It reminds me of early beach swims there, before shooting. When the sun was just coming up and the water was cool and I could start the day all alone, the horizon expanding out beside me.

I see Jordan on that beach. I blink him away.

"Paige'll be at the MTV Movie Awards," Alexis says, changing the subject.

"Your first awards show. Exciting," Georgina says, flicking some water at me. "It's such a scene."

"It's a scene when I go to Starbucks," I say.

Georgina laughs. "Some people have to pay for that kind of press," she says.

"Pay?"

Alexis cuts in. "Some people in Hollywood—no one in this pool, obviously—" The girls laugh at this. "But *some* people will tell photographers when they're going to be somewhere to make sure they get their picture snapped."

"Why?"

"Keeps you relevant," Georgina says, ducking under the water. She comes back up. "No offense, Paige, but you gotta work on your pap shots. You look like you want to murder someone every time I see you in a tabloid."

"I know," I say. "I'm trying." The press has taken to occasionally calling me "PG for Pained Grimace." It's not exactly something I'm proud of. It just feels like if I smile for them, if I play along, it means I'm saying that my life is theirs for the taking. How much do I owe people? How much access do they deserve?

"Are you coming back for the awards?" Alexis asks Georgina.

Georgina hoists herself out of the pool and flops down next to me, closing her eyes up to the sun. "Oh yeah. Although I'm really sick of winning TV couple without Blake. I look like an idiot up there."

"How does he consistently get out of everything?" Alexis asks.

"Because he never did it to begin with," Georgina answers. She pops her head up and looks at me. "Just remember this: what you do in the beginning is what they make you do in the middle. And the middle is long. The middle is the whole thing."

Alexis tops off my glass. "Paige doesn't have a choice," she says, handing it back to me. "Plus," Alexis says, waving me off. "You have Rainer on your arm—you're Young Hollywood's reigning queen. You might as well enjoy it while it lasts."

While it lasts. That's one thing they don't tell you: that built into every anxiety-riddled moment of fame is the very clear reminder that one day this blinding light will fade. It should make me feel relieved, but it doesn't.

I imagine stepping out of a car with Rainer, onto a carpet, like we did so many times on tour. People screaming. The world going nuts for every single move that we make, every smile we send each other's way. I don't think there is any way to get used to it. I think you would be crazy if you did.

"Yeah, we're talking about new projects," I venture.

"Wonderful!" Alexis says. "Tell me."

Georgina sighs. "You lucky bitch."

I blink at her. Alexis jumps in: "Forgive her jealousy."

"Television is brutal," Georgina continues. "I have like three weeks off a year."

Alexis pats her head. "We know, lovey." Then back to me. "Paige, you were saying?"

I shrug. "I don't know. I mean, there's a lot of stuff." My heart beats fast. I don't want to sound ungrateful. "I'm in a really lucky position. But the one thing I want . . ."

"They don't think you should do," Georgina says.

"Yes!" I say, sitting up.

"It's pretty normal," Georgina says. "They'll want you to follow a really specific trajectory, now. What does Rainer say?"

Alexis waves a dismissive hand. "Rainer only listens to his reps." She looks at me. "Right?"

I nod. "Yeah. And he wants me to, too." Rainer and I have had many conversations about how I should follow

Sandy and my agent's lead. "It's their job," Rainer always tells me. "Let them do it."

"Well it's worked for him," Alexis says. "But if you ask me he should have hit this level a long time ago."

"Yeah but his dad didn't produce *The Hunger Games*." Georgina glances at me. "Sorry," she says. "He's talented. Everyone knows that."

"I guess I'm just trying to figure out what's worth fighting for," I say.

Alexis puts her arms around me. "That's why you have us. It's important to have people in this business you can run stuff by and trust."

Trust. I'm not sure I do.

"Cassandra and Jake seemed nice," Alexis says to me.

I sit up a little straighter. There is something in her tone I don't like. "They're my best friends."

Alexis looks sideways at Georgina. Georgina bites her lip. "Things change when you become famous," Georgina says.

I don't respond, but I feel protective. I tuck my arms to my chest.

"We're just saying to be careful," Alexis says. "You'd be surprised who the press can get to. People who don't understand what it's like sometimes will see an opportunity . . ."

"The only thing Jake wants is for me to donate more

money to charities," I say, cutting her off. "Maybe your friends didn't get it, but you don't know mine."

Georgina shrugs. "Airport in an hour," she says. "I need to shower. You guys are welcome to stay."

Alexis gives her a sympathetic look. "Two more years," she says.

Georgina exhales. "I know. I can't wait. I told Blake if he even looks over those extended contracts we're breaking up. I can't play a teenage alien anymore. Even two more years is ridiculous. I'm starting to get wrinkles."

I look at her perfectly tanned, perfectly made-up face. Wasn't she in the pool? How does she still look impeccable? "I don't see any wrinkles," I say. "Anyway, I should head back." I have a bad taste in my mouth from this conversation, and I'm eager to see Rainer.

"No chance," Alexis says. "We're hitting up Robertson."

"I don't . . ."

"Know how to take a proper photograph? I know, and I'm going to teach you." Alexis and Georgina look at me. I feel their eyes travel from my chipped toenails up to my hair—held up with a ponytail holder. I pull it over my shoulder protectively.

"They're going to come after you any way you cut it," Georgina says. "You might as well stack the deck in your favor."

Georgina leaves and Alexis and I go to lunch at The

Ivy, this fancy restaurant on Robertson I gather celebrities go to get photographed. Charles Rider is sitting two tables over with the girl he left his wife for. He's been a major Hollywood player for twenty years and yet the paparazzi are barely even *pretending* to acknowledge him. All they care about is us.

Alexis never breaks a smile.

"Arch your back," she says. It makes your waist look smaller and your top look bigger. And don't smile with your teeth. It never turns out well."

I do as I'm told. I pick up my water glass. "Stop," Alexis says. "Hold the glass to your lips. Now put it down and wet your lips." I hear the flashes go off. "Good. Hand through your hair." Alexis shakes her mane out. I do the same with significantly less success.

"Now just talk," Alexis encourages. "Be normal."

Normal. I look down at my chopped salad, something not on the menu that Alexis ordered for me. I'm beginning to understand that there is an L.A. behind the L.A.—one comprised of unlisted menu items, back rooms, and secret doors. Things only accessible, seen, by a select few—*us*.

"Trying," I say, through my teeth.

"Relax your jaw," Alexis says. "That's where that nickname is coming from. You look like you're ready to clock me."

"Maybe I am," I say.

She smiles at me. "Don't be so neurotic. They can't hear us."

She's right. They're not too far away for photos but they are too far for sound.

"We haven't really had any time to get to know each other," she says. "I thought we could both use some girl talk."

"*Now?*"

"Why not?" She winks at me. "It's good practice for you. You need to start to learn how to hold your own when you're not tucked under Rainer's wing. Don't get me wrong, he's a great accessory, but you're not a package deal."

I bristle at this. It's not her right to judge how and in what way I'm dealing. Plus, the last thing I feel like doing is sharing girl talk with her in front of the paparazzi. Sit here, be photographed with lettuce in my teeth, and talk to her about 101-degree, scorching-hot sex with Jordan Wilder? Pass.

"You know I'm friends with Britney," she says before I have a chance to share any of this.

I cough on my water. She flicks her eyes upward. "I've known her forever. Since I was twelve, maybe."

Despite playing my younger sister in *Locked,* Alexis is actually a full four years older than me. But I'm beginning to see in Hollywood that doesn't mean much. Friendships are determined more by what age you play, than what age you are.

"Were you on *Backsplash*?" I ask. *Backsplash* was the TV show Rainer and Jordan and Britney were on as kids. It's how they all met, and became friends.

Alexis shakes her head. "No, but I knew her then. I knew them together." She looks at me but I can't quite read her expression.

I think about what Georgina said at her house. About Britney not being there for them.

"She's not a bad person," Alexis continues. "I mean, she's just not a very good one, either."

"It must be hard," I say, picking up my knife and absent-mindedly spreading some butter on a piece of bread. "I can't imagine going through something like this in such a public way."

"How is Rain doing?"

"You mean with his dad?"

Alexis nods.

"I'm not sure," I start. I've been so cautious of this, him, of what I say. But I know he's not totally himself. Rainer has always wanted to protect me, but now it's like he wants to protect me from *him*. Which is crazy. The whole point of uniting ourselves in front of the world was so that we could support each other, help each other. "He hasn't been sharing much with me," I say, cautiously.

Alexis perches her sunglasses on top of her head. Her eyes are golden, highlighted by the faintest hint of liner. "That must be hard," she says.

"I don't know why he thinks he has to do it on his own," I say. "He has it in his head he's protecting my image or something," I shrug. "I don't know."

"I get that," Alexis says. She tilts her head, thoughtful. "That's Rain. He's always going to put you first."

"I don't want to be first," I say. "I just want to be *with* him."

Alexis smiles. "You should tell him that."

"I have." Haven't I? I move my hands back and forth in front of us, clearing the air. "Ugh, enough." And then I take a deep breath. *Just ask, Paige. You can do it.* "How is it going with Jordan?"

Alexis seems happy to turn the conversation towards herself. She throws her head back. "Amazing!"

Her enthusiasm stings.

"He's a good guy," I say, wondering if my expression will give me away. I don't want a Paige Gives Good Bitchface headline on Fansugar tomorrow. Especially because the whole point of this adventure is to work on my public image.

She laughs. "Good guy? He's unbelievable. After everything he's been through with his family, you know? He's so strong. And of course the chemistry between us is . . . well, you know . . . the same as it is with you and Rainer, I bet!"

I know. I know what it feels like to be seen by Jordan, to be at the center of his universe, if only for a moment. Raw. Consuming. Maybe that wasn't me and Jordan. Maybe that's just Jordan, with everyone.

I take an extra bite of salad.

"Anyway." Alexis spears a chopped piece of asparagus. "I need an espresso." She makes a move to flag down the waiter and slides down a platinum credit card before I can argue.

"I'd like us to be friends," she says, quite abruptly.

"I thought we were."

She clears her throat. When she looks at me, I see her expression is thoughtful. "I'm not sure you like me."

I open my mouth to respond, but she holds up her hand. "I'm totally okay with that. For now. I don't mean to call you out. I know it's weird, being thrust into this universe as suddenly as you have been. I just want you to know *I* like you. I think you're genuine, which is hard to find in this town."

I put my elbows on the table. I want to ask her if she is, but instead I just say, "Thanks, I think."

"Can I just say something then, as your soon-to-be friend?"

I look at her. Hair perfectly windblown. White jeans

and crop top expertly draped over her tiny, toned frame. I want to hate her, but I can't. "No good sentence ever started with 'can I just say something.'"

She smiles. "I think you need to start having a little more fun. Come out of Rainer's shadow. You're living a dream and you act sometimes like it's a nightmare."

I think about getting defensive, but what would be the point? "It's that obvious?"

"You've seen the headlines."

I nod. "I have a photo shoot for the cover of *Vanity Fair*," I tell her. "And an interview with *Elle*. Plus all the awards-show prep . . ." I never in a million years thought these sentences would come out of my mouth (and my life).

Her spirits seem to lift right along with her forehead. She downs the espresso the waiter gives her and signs the credit card receipt in the same swoop. "And?"

"Will you help me pick out some stuff to wear?"

A smile so big I think it might break lights up her face. "Oh, PG," she says, "I thought you'd never ask."

CHAPTER 5

I come home with over ten shopping bags. Kitson, Reiss, Nanette Lapore. Dresses, sky-high heels and one leather bomber jacket Alexis insisted was "absolutely edible."

I'm already envisioning trying the stuff on for Rainer. He likes fashion. I'm not sure he'd cop to it, but I know he has a personal shopper. Clothes show up at the house, he tries them on, keeps some, and sends the rest back.

"Rainer?"

No answer, but his car is in the driveway. He must be home.

I set the bags down in the entryway. Maybe he's out by the pool.

"Rainer?"

I hear his voice coming from the bedroom—

unexpectedly animated, and angry. He's standing by the window holding his phone to his ear, and before I can announce myself, he barks into it.

"You're not listening to me, so let me be very clear: I know I once did your bidding but not now. That's not what this is about anymore."

He's quiet for a moment. Through the crackling silence I hear another voice on the other end of the line. His father. I'm not sure if I should walk away; our privacy is such a precious commodity these days . . . even Rainer is entitled to it. But I'm glued to the door. My breath is trapped in my lungs.

"I swear if you even come within a mile of her so help me God I'll kill you."

He hangs up the phone, slamming it against the desk so hard it makes me jump out of my flip-flops. My gasp gives me away and Rainer looks up, his face immediately retreating from rage to surprise.

"Sorry," I blurt out, shifting my weight in the doorway. "I couldn't find you, and by the time I got here—"

He freezes for a moment. Even his hand doesn't move. But his eyes quickly dart away from me. "I'm sorry you had to hear that."

I want to go to him, to hug him, but he feels closed off somehow. This stuff with his family is bigger than I thought, and for the first time I consider that maybe it is powerful enough to come between us. "That's okay," I said. "Is he threatening your mom?" I ask.

"What?"

"You said if you come within a mile of her . . ." My voice trails off.

Rainer is looking at the floor. "Oh, yeah."

I pause for a moment, deciding whether to press the issue. "I didn't—I didn't realize it had gotten that bad." I didn't realize we were keeping things from each other, is what I want to say, but I hold the words back.

He doesn't answer and when he makes a move to stand I instinctively thrust my bags at him. "I went shopping," I say, trying a different tactic. Maybe distracting him will help. "With Alexis. Want to check out my loot?"

He glances at me absent-mindedly. "Maybe in a bit."

I look down at the desk and realize there are papers strewn all over it. "What are you doing?"

He exhales then, long. "I was trying to read through my mom's divorce papers."

"Oh, Rainer." I go over to him. I rub his neck.

He shakes his head. "People are coming out of the woodwork, now. His old assistant, one studio exec." He runs a hand over his eyes. "It's too much. I can't blame her."

"When did she decide?"

He shrugs. "The last few days? I don't know, Paige. I've

been distracted." I feel him flinch away from my fingertips. Rainer never gets short with me.

I think about tour, my birthday last night. "We've been working," I say, unsure of the words, whether they're true. Have I been distracting him?

"Yeah, but this is my family."

I can feel my skin behind my eyes burning and I turn to leave when I feel his hands reach for me. In the next breath he's pulling me down into his lap.

"I'm sorry," he says, the side of his face pressed to mine. "I just . . ."

"It's okay," I say. "You don't need to apologize."

"I love you," he says, suddenly.

I know he does. I've known it since the premiere, maybe longer, but hearing it now, like this, is new. We've never said it. Not directly. Not with nothing standing in between the words.

He runs a hand up and down my back. "You don't have to say anything," he says. "I just . . . I just needed you to know."

"I love you too," I say. Automatically, without thought.

"You do?"

I nod my head. I place both my hands on either side of his face. "Rainer, of course I do."

He kisses me then. Parting my lips with his own.

I think back to his reaction on the phone just now.

"What does your father want you to do?" I ask.

Rainer's arms tighten around me. "Nothing I'm willing to," he says.

I thread my fingers through his hair. He closes his eyes, pulling me tighter. "I can't lose you," he says suddenly.

I turn his face back to mine. "Why would you even say that?" I ask. "Of course you're not going to lose me. Rainer, I'm right here."

He buries his head in my neck. I wrap my arms around him and kiss everywhere I can reach with my lips. "I love you," I repeat.

I think about that moment on the cliffs of Ho'okipa all those months ago. We made promises to each other. We said we'd be there. I don't know why he doesn't understand, after all this time, that it works both ways.

The next morning we have a rehearsal for the MTV awards. Rainer and I arrive at six AM and are shuffled through stage directions. Jordan is there, too, and the two of them are cordial bordering, maybe, on friendly. At one point Rainer even brings Jordan a cup of coffee and Jordan comments on how Rainer still remembers how he likes it—black (of course).

I hang with Alexis, who spends the morning coaching Georgina through some drama with Blake. At least she's not loving up Jordan.

As soon as they stop moving us around the stage like little chess pieces, Rainer has to go.

"I thought we were having lunch?" I ask him.

"Mom needs me," he says, pulling me in for a quick kiss. "Are you ready? I'll drop you off first."

One of the producers shakes her head. "We need Paige for another twenty. Sorry, guys."

Rainer looks at his watch. "Damn. I guess I could leave the car with you?"

I wave him off. "No need, I'll call a taxi."

Rainer looks unconvinced. "You sure?"

"Yes," I say, planting a kiss on his lips. "Go."

Actually, they only need me for another five once they realize Alexis is gone. I could have told them that. She left an hour ago with Georgina. I got a text from her that said: *Sry. Burning Blake's things. Plans tonight?*

Alexis and I were supposed to present together but they trade us out for two others. Fine by me. It's one less thing I have to think about on award's night.

I'm about to call a car when I see Jordan still standing there, talking to one of the show's hosts. He catches my eye and excuses himself. I fiddle with my phone in my hands as my nervous system starts to scramble.

"Rainer take off?" he asks.

"Yeah, he had to . . ." I let my voice trail off. "Family stuff."

Jordan nods. "I can drop you off, if you want?" It's a question, but the intonation in his voice doesn't change.

I slip my phone back into my bag. "That would be great."

Jordan shoves his hands into his pockets. "Cool. Any interest in food?"

As if on cue, my stomach rumbles. It's noon, I've been up since five, and all I've had was a stale croissant from the craft service they put out.

"Yes," I say. "I'm starving."

Jordan cocks his head for me to follow him. We sneak up the aisle and then around to the back of the theater where his truck is parked. I get in and he immediately starts speeding away.

"Where should we go?" I ask, pretending like we have unlimited options, like we could just stroll into Nobu and eat in the window.

"I've got it covered," Jordan says. He glances at me, and then away, back at the traffic ahead. I roll down the window and let my hand trail out beside me. I'm remembering our morning climbing up Haleakala in his car, the air growing colder, me curled up in his sweatshirt. It feels like decades ago now and yet it's here, right now. Sitting in the center console between us.

We arrive at a Mexican restaurant called El Cholo, situated between a gas station and a convenience store.

Jordan parks in the lot and then motions for me to follow him through the heavy metal doors. Inside the restaurant is expansive, so no one really notices us. A man comes up and claps Jordan on the back.

"Santiago," Jordan says. "How are you?"

"It has been a long time," Santiago says.

"Hey," I cut in.

"This is Paige," Jordan says, gesturing to me.

Santiago smiles warmly and pulls me in for a kiss on the cheek. "Beautiful," he says. Jordan raises his eyebrows.

"She's taken," he says. There's no irony in his tone.

"Too bad," Santiago says. "But I have a perfect table for you. This way." Santiago takes us through the main room into a booth in the back. "Guacamole on the way."

"Thanks, man," Jordan says.

"I take it you come here often?" I ask when Santiago dashes off.

"Once in a while," Jordan says, his eyes on mine.

"So what's good?" I ask, fumbling with the menu. I can feel my heartbeat under my T-shirt. The cotton is doing little to hide what's going on inside me from being this close, this *alone,* with Jordan.

"The green tamales," Jordan says. "Just trust me on this one."

Santiago returns with the promised guacamole and I dive into the chip basket. Jordan gives me a smile.

"Careful," he says. "You're going to choke. I'm not really in the mood to perform CPR."

"Wouldn't be the first time."

I shake my head, remembering the day he rescued me from drowning in the ocean on Maui. I swam out too far and he pulled me in, practically brought me back to life.

Jordan takes a sip of water. Why did I have to say that? Stupid.

"So how are you?" he asks. In the sunlight I see his scar behind his ear—a reminder of so many things. It seems to wink at me, like we're in on some secret.

"Pretty good," I say. "I mean, it's weird, all of this."

"Yeah."

"I guess I'll get used to it."

He shrugs. "Maybe." He unclips his sunglasses from where they hang off his shirt and sets them on the table.

I thread my napkin through my fingers. It feels like when I first met Jordan. How it was like pulling teeth, getting him to have a conversation. "How are you?" I ask.

"Good," he says. "I've been seeing a lot of my sister."

"Oh yeah? How is she?"

Jordan laughs. It makes my body relax. "Starting high school," he says.

"Yikes."

"She knows if she dates before she's thirty I'll ground her for life, though, so we're all good."

"Seems reasonable."

"What about your sister? Deep in wedding planning?"

He remembers. "Oh yeah," I say. "She's been sending me all kinds of crazy requests lately."

"Pitfalls of stardom," Jordan says.

"I think just pitfalls of sisterhood, actually."

Jordan laughs. "You're not looking forward to it at all?"

"No, I am." I'm hesitant to go home. What will it be like? Last time I was home was before the movie came out. I'm just not entirely sure I belong there anymore, or what it will be like once I'm back. "It's just weird. Balancing this life with that one."

Jordan runs a hand over his chin. He's quiet for a moment, then he looks at me, like really looks at me. "So how are you doing being back? Besides getting stalked on Robertson, I mean."

I think about my planned paparazzi shoot with Alexis. He saw that?

"I don't know," I say. "Good, I guess."

I know he's asking about Rainer and I, but I'm not sure I can talk about it with him. What would I say? *Great, Jordan, Rainer told me he loved me last night. Thanks for asking!*

"I hung out with Georgina and Alexis yesterday," I offer instead. I silently pray he won't elaborate on her.

I don't think I can bear hearing about their chemistry from him.

But he doesn't react, or offer information. Instead he leans forward, snagging a tortilla chip, and asks what he wants to know, so there's no way out. "How is Rainer?"

I think about my options. Telling him he's great. And part of that would be true. But Jordan cares about Rainer. I know he asks because he really wants to know. And more than anything, after so many lies, I want to be honest with him. If we're going to be friends, maybe we could start here.

"It has been pretty hard on him," I confess. I don't tell him about the divorce, or last night, his heated words with his father.

"It's tough," Jordan says. "I feel for him."

I see a vein in his neck flinch, and I know he means it. Jordan has his own family drama. He knows what it's like to live out such a personal saga in such a public way.

I wish they could talk to each other. I've seen them be friendlier, but it's clear Jordan is still maintaining his distance. And I feel responsible. It's my fault they're not friends now. And I don't have any idea what to do to fix it.

"He doesn't want anything to do with his father," I say.

Jordan nods. "Greg used to have a pretty big hold on Rainer. He's always done what his father asked, no matter what." He looks right at me when he says it, and something about the intensity in his eyes makes me stop. It's like he's trying to communicate with them—to fill in something that his words cannot. "Just don't be surprised if the tables turn again."

"Turn on what?"

Jordan sighs, wraps his hands around his water glass. "If he goes back to being Greg's son."

"Jordan, Britney was his girlfriend. I don't see how he could forgive that."

Jordan clears his throat. He has the slightest evidence of a five o'clock shadow. It makes him look older. It's strange. Rainer has three years on Jordan but Jordan has always appeared older to me. Rainer still has a childlike innocence. Or he used to, anyway.

"It's his father," Jordan says.

I think about Jordan's own father—the scar on his face, the public financial battles. Jordan would never forgive him. He would never let his father back in. And for a moment I don't know which is better.

"Maybe," I reply, because I'm not sure what else to say.

Our food arrives. Sizzling plates of tamales. They taste as good as they look.

"So what's next?" he asks. I think for a second he's talking about us, but then he quickly clarifies. "Have you signed on to any other projects?"

"There's one I want," I say between bites. "*Closer to Heaven.*"

For the first time all day, I see Jordan really smile. "Kick ass script," he says. "They want you for India?"

I nod. "Well, sorta. I want me for India."

"You gotta do it."

"Trust me, I know. Sandy doesn't seem that psyched about it. And they're not into me for the part." I take another cheesy bite.

Jordan looks like he's heard me wrong. He sits back and squints. "You're kidding, right?"

"Nope," I say. "I'm too blockbuster or something." I shrug. "I asked to meet with the writers and director, we'll see if it happens."

"We'll see?" Jordan shakes his head. "Paige, this is *your* career. Not Sandy's, not your agent's, not Tawny's, not even that director's. If you want this, you need to go after it."

I swallow. Rainer says the reason I have reps is so that they can make these decisions for me, but I don't say that. It feels stupid to parrot Rainer, especially to Jordan.

He looks at me. Hard. "Do you want this?"

I study his jaw. The curve of his face. "More than anything," I say.

"So fight," Jordan says. "Show them you can do it. Don't take no for an answer." He leans forward, close, and instinctively I put my hands on the table, right by his elbows. I want to curl my fingers around his wrists, grab on to his arms. I feel the need to touch him—like it's another limb all its own.

Jordan eyes my hands and then sits up. "We should head back," he says.

The subtle rejection stings. I want to protest—just ten more minutes—but I know it wouldn't make a difference. There is so much I want to say to him, none of which he should hear.

"Alexis waiting for you?" I ask. It comes out accusatory, and I mentally kick myself.

"We're going to a premiere tonight. The new Scorsese," he says, side-stepping the question.

"Cool."

We look at each other. We both know I'm lying.

He looks at me another beat—long enough for me to want to ask him how we ended up here. Barely scraping the surface. I remember once being closer to him than anyone. And now—

Jordan barely talks on the way home and when he drops me off he doesn't get out.

"Nice to see you," he says.

"I'll see you at the awards, I guess?"

Jordan nods. It seems sad, slightly. "Best kiss," he says. "Right." We glance at each other.

"At least we won't win," he says. And then he's gone.

CHAPTER 6

The MTV Movie Awards are upon us. We're up for six. Best female performance, best male performance for Rainer and Jordan, movie of the year, best kiss—twice, in case anyone has forgotten. And I haven't. The idea of having to banter with Rainer on that stage in front of Jordan and the world is making me scan this limo for a possible exit strategy.

I'm sitting in the back, a silver dress on, and leopard-print heels I have zero idea how I'm going to walk in. I tried to get the stylist to let me wear flats, but the conversation pretty much just went like: *no*.

Tawny is chattering on her cell, and Sandy is deep in conversation with Rainer. He's sitting next to me, his hand in mine. I know I'm gripping a little too tightly. Half because of the nerves, and half because this is the most I've seen him all week.

He's been sleeping at his mom's a lot. It freaks me out how freaked out I am to be without him. It used to be that on the rare occasion I got the house to myself it was absolute heaven. In Portland, I would have spent all of my savings for one night alone in the Townsen house. And now? Now I think about paparazzi finding me. I think about the millions of fans on the internet whose happiness seems to be dependent on our staying together. Being alone makes me feel like I'm being pulled under by them.

"She told him he should resign, but he won't," Rainer is saying to Sandy. They're discussing Greg.

I look out the window at the approaching theater. The fans are gathered outside—throngs of them. Lights and noise and somewhere—Jordan.

Alexis and I went to Georgina's beach house a few days ago. Georgina wasn't there—she's in Atlanta filming. We hung by the pool and took a walk on the beach. I told her a little about Rainer, and she listened. I was surprised, unnerved, actually, at how easy it was to talk to her. I'm still not sure how much I can trust her, but she also happens to be my only friend here. As much as my daily phone calls with Cassandra keep me sane, there are things that no matter how hard I try to explain, she just can't understand.

"Just remember you're gonna get a lot of camera time.

So don't mess with your dress and make sure to keep your face neutral."

It takes me a moment to realize Sandy is talking to me. I nod. "Yeah," I say. "I got it."

"I know," she says. "You're my old pro now." She winks at me.

I know the camera will cut away to us constantly. People are watching to see our reactions—to the awards, to each other. I've seen the videos they have on YouTube of us—compiled footage from press tour and the movie—trying to make some kind of romantic narrative set to a medley of Coldplay songs. Some of them are kind of sweet. Like my own personal home video, or something.

It is, of course, tradition that the people who win Best Kiss kiss onstage. We've already rehearsed a Best Kiss bit. Rainer is going to grab me and lift me up and in the moment before our lips touch he's going to carry me offstage. Keep them wanting more, our fun motto.

My cell phone rings and I take my hand out of Rainer's. Alexis's name flashes on the screen.

"Hey," I say. "We're just a few blocks away. Are you there?"

I'm met with a rattling cough. "Darling," she croaks back.

"Jesus. You sound like death. Are you okay?"

Her voice is thick and weak through the phone. "I have the plague. I'm not going to make tonight."

I feel my nerves tighten up. Alexis had promised to walk the carpet next to me. She was supposed to sit with the three of us.

"I'm sorry," she continues. "But you've got your boyfriend." More coughing. The phone goes silent and I wait to hear her voice.

"Alexis?"

"Sorry. Yes. I wish I could be there. I actually like these things. But it's just not possible. Green phlegm is not ideal for my reputation."

I shake my head. "Of course. Rest up. We'll miss you."

"I'll talk to you tomorrow," she says, then hangs up in a flurry of nasal noises.

"Everything okay?" Rainer is sitting next to me, looking from my face to the phone.

"Alexis is sick. She's not going to come," I say, slipping my hand back into his.

Tawny puts her palm over the voice pad of her cell. "Jordan," she mouths to us.

"They weren't going to walk together, anyway," Rainer says to her. Then, to me: "Were they?"

I shrug. "I have no idea. Jordan isn't really in the habit of telling me that stuff."

Rainer clears his throat. "It didn't come up at lunch?" He looks at me when he says it and I feel my hand turn to lead in his.

I exhale slowly. "You mean after rehearsal?" I quickly remember that I told Rainer Jordan dropped me off. He didn't seem to care. It's not like anything happened.

But Rainer isn't accusing me of anything now. He suspected something was going on with us at the end of filming, but once Jordan told him the truth about his father, he let it all go. And to Rainer's credit, he hasn't brought up my relationship with Jordan since. Sometimes I don't understand how he can be so big about the whole thing.

He rolls his neck. "I thought maybe he opened up. He's been pretty tight-lipped about her."

"Trust me," I say. "He's not telling me anything he's not telling you."

Our limo begins to slow and the familiar sensation of nerves, excitement and panic blooms in my stomach. It's amazing to meet fans, to feel their love and passion for *Locked*. It's just scary to see so many of them at once. Rainer lets go of my hand. "You ready?" he asks.

"Yep," I say, trying on my best and brightest smile.

"Can you guys please make an effort to not look so fucking miserable?" Tawny asks from the other end of the limo.

We both look at her. Tawny is a pest, but she's usually more annoyingly chirpy than lecturing. And she doesn't swear. I'm taken aback.

"You look like you've been shot up with multiple

infectious diseases," she finishes.

Rainer looks at me. "I think you look hot," he says. "But I'm not a professional."

Tawny chucks her phone on the seat. "I think it's time you two engaged in some PDA."

Sandy crosses her arms. She raps on the driver's window. "We need a minute," she says. To Tawny: "What are you suggesting?"

Tawny leans forward. She's so thin I can see the veins working overtime in her neck. "It's been a rough few weeks. Rainer's stock is down. This thing with your father has not been great for your image."

Rainer's jaw tightens. "My image? Sorry I didn't consult with you before my dad tried to fuck my ex."

Sandy and I look at each other like *whoa* but Tawny doesn't bite. "But you *should* have consulted me before you outed him in front of one of the world's nosiest reporters."

I hold up my hands. "Okay," I say. "What do you want from us?"

"Show the world you're united. That you're standing by your man. He needs it."

Rainer shakes his head. "Jesus Christ," he says.

I look at Rainer. "Do you . . ."

"I could kill him," he says.

"I know. But hey, he's not here. It's just us. What do you want to do?" I lay my fingertips on his shoulder.

His face softens. He leans over and touches my cheek. "Wanna hold my hand?"

I take his fingers and twine them through mine. "Always," I say.

Sandy clears her throat. "Save it for the cameras," she says. "Get out there."

They always go nuts when we step out of the car, but the combined impact of being together, and holding hands, sends them over the edge. We're giving them what they want and our fans totally freak the hell out. The screams feel like they're going to blow out my eardrums. But it's so much better with Rainer next to me. I'm feeling confident, with his hand in mine. More in my element than I have been in a while. I sign autographs. I pose for pictures. A few girls start to cry and Rainer and I give them a group hug.

We make our way down the carpet. I spot Josh Horwart, a journalist for MTV who interviewed us all in London. I really liked him, and I know a lot of celebrities have become friendly with him. He's just chilled. Very few journalists treat you like you're a normal human being, not a bug in a jar—and he's definitely one of them.

"Hey, guys," he says when we reach him. "How's it going?"

"Hey, man," Rainer says. "Pretty good."

Josh doesn't ask about Rainer's father or our

relationship. Instead he asks us if we're excited to be repping *Locked* at our first awards show.

"You forget the MTV award I won for *Backsplash*," Rainer says.

"Oh right. What was that? Adolescent Hottie?"

I laugh. "He's up for the same thing tonight."

Rainer slips an arm around me. The crowds shriek. "She's just bitter she didn't get nominated."

I mock-glare at him and we say goodbye to Josh.

We're in a groove. The rest of the carpet goes about the same.

E online: What was your pre-awards show prep like today?"

Rainer: basketball and a shower.

Me: My look took a little more effort.

Rainer: Don't believe her. She wakes up this way.

I nudge him, he kisses my cheek.

Once we're in our seats—dead center, front row—Rainer's light dims considerably. I've seen it happen before. He's such high-wattage on carpets—all laughs and smiles—that he burns out once it's over. He immediately orders a Jack and diet. The waiter asks if they can bring me anything. I'm about to shake my head when I say champagne. I expect them to turn me down. I mean they know I'm not twenty-one (there have been endless tabloid stories about the age gap between Rainer and me), but they bring it to me immediately.

My head is feeling fuzzy by the time the show starts. Between the champagne in the limo and here, I feel light, disoriented. Considerably less nervous, though. And that's when Jordan slides into the seat next to me. His shoulder brushes mine. "Sorry I'm late," he whispers.

He's so close I can smell him—a warm mix of sea and land. Salt water and dirt and cinnamon, too. That's new. Probably Alexis's influence. I imagine her gifting him expensive cologne. I feel myself flush and will the image out of my head. Alexis is my friend. Jordan is my friend. *Stop, Paige.*

"Sorry Alexis is sick," I whisper.

Jordan doesn't respond.

Rainer takes my hand.

I feel them both next to me. I don't think I'll ever get used to having Jordan on one side, and Rainer on the other. I feel like my heart wants to rip in half just so they'll both have a piece. I know the camera will catch Rainer and I touching. *Raige-ingly in Love.*

Jeremy Brown is hosting—he's the guy from the mockumentary show about the crazy Midwest family—and he comes onto the jumbo-tron. He's in front of what's obviously a green-screen that is projecting a beach. All palm trees and sand. They're going to do a spoof of *Locked.* They didn't show us this in rehearsals—it was probably after we all took off.

Terror grips me right along with Rainer's hand. The camera is going to be on us the whole time. "If you get nervous, just smile," Tawny told me. "No one ever ruined their rep by being happy." She eyed me when she said it. I know she has been annoyed about the pissed-off vibe I'm sporting in the tabloids.

I try it. I feel like a chipmunk.

For the opening, Penelope and Ryan, the stars of the Disney show about Witches, are wandering around stage. Penelope is in a coconut bra.

"I'm just so torn," she says. "Who should I be with? The crazy guy who wants me to live with him on a deserted island with no HBO, or the one who just brought a private jet to rescue me? There is no clear winner."

"We're right here, you can just talk to us," Ryan says. He's dressed like Rainer's Noah, down to the linen pants. "Stop doing voice over."

"Seriously, guys, I don't have time for love triangles right now. We have to go. I'm supposed to be hosting the MTV Movie Awards in like ten minutes," Jeremy says.

Penelope looks at her watch. "Actually, you're supposed to be hosting them now."

Jeremy and Penelope exchange panicked looks, but Ryan just crosses his arms. "Chill, you're on island time, dude."

Jeremy looks at Penelope, cocks his thumb. "What do you see in this guy?"

Penelope looks at the audience before lifting up Ryan's shirt. She points to his perfect six-pack.

"Fair enough," Jeremy says.

"Where is this jet?" Penelope asks. "Is it here?"

Jeremy puts his hands on Penelope's hips. "Yeah, it's here. Can we stop talking and get the heck on it?"

Ryan steps between them. "She loves me—she's staying. This is just your ploy to get her to leave with you."

"It's totally working," Penelope says dreamily.

Ryan looks at the audience and then looks at Penelope. "Screw it, I'm coming with you."

"Great, fine. Whoever's coming, it's now or never." A bunch of people dressed in tribal gear rush towards the helicopter on stage.

"To the MTV Movie Awards!" Jeremy calls.

The screen goes black and everyone starts applauding. Then the three of them appear out of the video, and onstage.

Jeremy waves to the audience. "Welcome to the MTV Movie Awards!" he bellows. Penelope is smiling next to him. She looks delighted—totally excited and happy to be up there. Ryan looks mildly bored.

"We'll be your hosts for the night and we promise to have some fun. But first, we have to mortify people." Jeremy looks right down at us. "So many of our favorites are here tonight. Rainer Devon is sitting front row!"

Rainer gives him a little salute.

"Sorry about that opening, Rainer," Penelope says.

Jeremy interrupts. "He gets to go home with Paige Townsen. Don't feel too badly for him."

The entire stadium screams. I want to crawl under my seat and die. I see Rainer laugh next to me and smile. I just put my hand over my forehead and shake my head.

"Seriously. Let's give it up for this trio. The stars of *Locked*, ladies and gentleman!"

Cheers and claps. I see Jordan's face on the screen— trying to smile. It barely passes for genuine.

They single out a few more people and then they start with the awards.

Grant Fisher wins the award for best on-screen villain. Apple Harrison wins for best female in a comedy. They're giving out best male lead in a drama. Rainer and Jordan are both nominated and when the camera pans to Jordan I see him give a small smile and tilt his head.

Then Rainer is up. He flashes on the screen next to me—calm and cool and collected.

"And the MTV Movie Award goes to . . ."

"Rainer Devon! For his portrayal of Noah in *Locked*."

Rainer stands next to me and I do the same, moving to hug him. He doesn't kiss me, thank God. Just a quick embrace and then he jogs forward, taking the stairs two at a time. He air-kisses the actress holding the popcorn statue and then takes the microphone.

"You guys are too good to me. This is awesome."

Everyone goes wild. I swear he could say anything right now; he could read a history textbook, and people would scream.

He's flashing his dimpled smile and shaking his head. "Settle down," he tells the crowd. "I just want to say how honored I am. Honestly. We do this thing for you guys and the fact that you love it means the world."

I think he's done, that he's about give them a little salute and walk offstage, but instead he tips his head down with his hand like a brim on his forehead. "PG?" he asks.

Time stops. I can feel every muscle in my body freeze up in preparation for impact.

"There are too many lights," he says. "But I just want to thank my brilliant co-star, Paige Townsen." The screams are hysterical. I am vaguely aware of my lips pulling into a smile. "I wouldn't be up here without her, and I think we all know that. Thank you, guys!"

The lights fade as he walks offstage, but I still feel out of my body. And I don't get put back in when the lights come up because Rainer is right back in his seat, taking my hand, the cameras on us, and they're introducing Tevin Black, a guy I know is friends with Rainer—some comedy actor—who is giving out the award for best kiss.

Here we go. We're about to have to get up there again—this time together. Best kiss. They go through the other couples first then end with both from *Locked*, the one with Rainer, and the one with Jordan.

They announce my name and I'm already standing, looking to Rainer. Let's just do this, get it over with. My hands feel numb by my sides and my insides feel like they're been strung up with live wire.

But then the craziest thing happens. They don't call Rainer's name. They call Jordan's.

I spin to look at him and he's just sitting there, bewilderment on his face. But in a split second it's gone, and he's standing, his hand on my lower back. "Come on," he whispers into my ear. "Let's go."

I don't look back at Rainer. He's a pro, though. If he's surprised, I know he wouldn't show it.

Standing onstage at an award's show is one of the most surreal experiences—and I've had a lot of them as of late. You know there are thousands of people there—millions watching—but you can't see anyone. It's too bright. It feels like looking out into a sea of kinetic energy. The air crackles with light, spark, *mania*.

We get up onstage and take our golden awards, shaped like popcorn in movie theater cups. They are heavier than they look on TV. Jordan flashes me a side smile and then takes the microphone. "Thanks, guys," he says. "I don't think we were expecting this." He's less assured than Rainer was up here. Jordan is different. Jordan told me once that to him it's not about the celebrity, it's about the work. We share that. Neither one of us knows how to deal. Which is why it sucks we're up here together.

But the crowd doesn't want us to talk. They don't want us to act, either. They're chanting. *Kiss. Kiss.*

Jordan looks at me again. His shoulders edge up, just slightly. And then everything seems to dim down. Almost fade entirely. I hear the crowd like a distant roar—far off, away. It's like standing outside a football stadium. The noise feels like it doesn't even belong to us.

My feet start moving towards him. I think about that day on the beach in Hawaii. About how he rolled me on top of him in the cabana in the rain. About how wonderful and terrible it felt—like the beginning and ending of everything, all at once. The dawn of the world in one single, blinding moment. But even that memory doesn't stick. Up here nothing seems to hold any weight. It's like being underwater.

I don't know how long it has been—mere milliseconds, probably—but I'm standing in front of him now. And he's looking at me in a way he hasn't in so long. He's looking at me in a way I don't dare think about, not even in my dreams.

"What do you think?" he says into the microphone, his eyes still on me.

I'm not sure what my face is doing, but I'm aware of my feet taking steps towards him. I'm aware of the moment stretching out—the air between us even more charged than it is around us. It's like we're in some vortex being pulled or pressed closer and closer. I can't tell what's drawing us together—ourselves, or the waves of screams and cries from the audience.

His hands drift to my waist. I tilt my face up to his. I look into his eyes. They're filled with questions, but I just answer the one. I reach up and loop my hands around his neck and then . . . we're kissing.

His lips land hard on my mouth, and I open them to him. My hands find his hair—they thread through. I want to touch him everywhere. I want to run my fingertips down his face. I want to memorize the milliseconds between the pulses in his neck. I want to be so close to him that even when this moment is over there will be enough to last.

I'm never allowed this, and the sheer torture of want—of being so close but not being able to simply reach up and lay my lips on his—bursts through the surface. Every impulse I've hidden. Every time I've wanted to put my head on his shoulder. To put my hand on his cheek. Every intimate gesture that's been pushed down, banished to where it came from, roars back with something close to vengeance. It feels like the world is going to break open from the sheer relief I feel at being able to kiss him.

I'm never going to be able to stop.

I feel myself reach for him, to pull him down even closer. To press my chest up against his and fit our bodies together so there is no space, not even an inch, but he pulls back and releases me.

The lack of contact makes me grope forward, but he has his hands on my shoulders and his eyes carry a warning— *no*.

I see his chest rise and fall. He holds my gaze for a beat, and then he's turning back to the crowd. The noise comes back all at once, like taking a blaring television off mute. People whoop, scream. Jordan speaks. "Er, hopefully that's what you were after. Thanks again."

Then his hand is on my arm and he's steering me backstage.

Four different people descend on us when we get there, but I shake my head, pushing past them. *Just one minute. Not now.* I follow Jordan into a corner.

"Christ," he says under his breath. "What the hell was that?"

I know there are a million people around, some of them hovering, waiting to move us like little chess pieces to our next location.

"What was what?" I say. "YOU kissed me."

He shakes his head. "We won best kiss, you kiss. It's a tradition. I wasn't trying to make out with you in front of

America. You—" He looks at me. Puts a fist to his forehead and holds it there.

"Then why did you do it?" I cross my arms. I suddenly feel naked in this dress. Anger flares up in my chest. "Why didn't you just say sorry and thank them and walk off the goddamn stage, Jordan?"

He drops his fist. His eyes find mine. He doesn't say anything but I see it there, right beneath the surface. He looks about as miserable as I feel.

"Jordan . . ." I start, gentler this time, but a girl with a headset is pointing to us and Rainer is walking over. He comes up behind Jordan and puts a hand on his shoulder.

"You guys make good TV."

"Tradition," Jordan mumbles.

Rainer reaches and pulls me towards him, planting a quick kiss on my cheek. "Congrats," he says.

There is no bitterness in his tone, no sarcasm, and for a minute this pisses me off more than Jordan yelling at me for kissing him back. Does Rainer not even care? Did he even *notice*?

"Hey," Rainer says. He cocks his head in the direction of the door. "There's someone I want you to meet."

"Don't you think we should get back to our seats?" I ask. I realize my voice is shaking. If that kiss looked like nothing to Rainer, then maybe it looked like nothing to the audience, too. I remember the bloopers reel from Hawaii.

How they played an extended scene of Jordan and my onscreen kiss and how Rainer immediately picked up on the fact that something was going on. How pissed he was. But now—nothing.

I still feel the champagne swirling around my head, but I try to let the rational thoughts march through, gather some order. 1) I should be happy that I'm not dating a crazy, jealous sociopath. 2) Rainer let all that Jordan stuff go for us. Why would I want to dredge it up again? Why would I want to hurt him? This kiss was just part of the job.

I glance at Jordan, but he's not looking at me. He's watching someone coming towards us. I follow his gaze to see a girl about my height. Dark skin, jet-black hair and razor-sharp green eyes. She's wearing a neon blue leather dress and her heels are sky-high but she walks with confidence. Totally assured, like she could run a marathon in them. Like maybe she will.

She reaches us and her eyes land on me. Her gaze is halting as she takes me in—down to the feet and then slow pan—up up up. I know who she is immediately. It makes me take a step back. The force of her: the girl who came before me. She drove Rainer and Jordan to hate each other. She commanded intense, limitless loyalty. She was the start of so much.

"Paige," Rainer says, his hand waving from her to me. "This is Britney Drake."

CHAPTER 7

Britney smiles with her mouth, but her eyes are too busy for emotion. She's studying me. And she doesn't put out her hand.

"Quite a performance you just put on," she says, her gaze flitting to Jordan. "I was impressed, Wilder."

Her voice is low, throaty. When she speaks, it's like she's playing an instrument—I can feel the sound waves cut through me.

I clear my throat. I can see where this interaction is going, and I won't let it. I'm not here to compete. "Britney," I say, mustering all the genuine-ness I can. "It's nice to finally meet you."

"Right. Anybody want a sip?" she says, turning her attention to the group and shaking a little bedazzled flask.

Her smile has turned to a smirk. I instantly feel like she's patronizing me.

Her eyes take in Rainer standing next to me and instinctively I snuggle closer to him. He looks down at me and smiles. If he's feeling awkward, he's not showing it. I know he's seen Britney before tonight. I know he did while we were apart, too. Not romantically. At least, that's what he said, and I believe him. Rainer wouldn't lie to me.

"This thing is winding down. Let's stay back here for Best Movie and then take off. I'm throwing an after party at the Roosevelt," Britney says, before looking back at me. "You're welcome to come, too, Paige, of course."

I barely register her dig at me before my thoughts all jumble together. What I want to do is go home and sleep. Be with Rainer. Have a little time to just *be*.

"Wilder?" Britney asks. "You in?"

"Nah, I'm gonna take off actually."

Britney sticks out her bottom lip. "Boo."

"Tend to the beautiful Alexis's sick bed?" Rainer says.

Jordan laughs. "Something like that."

I keep my eyes focused on Britney. I'm distinctly aware of her watching me. I have no idea what Jordan's relationship is like with Britney now. Are they still close friends? Do they talk? Has he told her about Alexis? Has he told her about me?

"Bye, Brit," Jordan says. He half waves at the group of us.

Rainer turns to me. "Roosevelt?" he asks.

"Rain," Britney coos, before I can respond. "You promised."

Rainer keeps looking at me. I reach down and take his hand. I make sure she sees. "Sure," I say, my eyes on hers. "Whatever you want."

An hour later Rainer and I are pulling up to the Roosevelt Hotel. I crouch down in the seat as we make a sharp left, avoiding the front, paparazzi-packed entrance and swing down an alley. We get taken into the private, underground garage and then we're led by two big bodyguards in through a secret door hidden inside a library bookcase. Then we go down a hallway of old Hollywood photographs into a huge Vaudeville theater. Red velvet benches, dim chandelier lighting, jumbo screens and a stage in the center where women are dancing with monkeys onstage. And to top it all off, waitresses are delivering bottles to people's tables— by flying through the air.

"This is insane," I say.

"It's pretty crazy, huh?" Rainer says. "But kinda fun. It's Britney's favorite place."

"How is she doing by the way?"

Rainer shakes his head. "It's worse for her," he says. "She's in the press constantly and it's all about Greg."

"Have you guys talked about it?"

"A little," he says. "She has a tendency to go off the rails a bit when things get rough,"

I think about Britney and her little flask of happy juice backstage at the MTV awards. The more unscrupulous tabloids have run a few stories about her drinking habit, her partying ways . . . but I just assumed they were exaggerations. Like Rainer and my movie-theater date or "promise" ring. But weren't there seeds of truth in those stories, too? Maybe Britney is in trouble.

"She wants us to be friends," Rainer says. I think about Britney's eyes on me backstage. Friends. Right. That's exactly what she wants from Rainer.

"What do you want?" I ask.

Rainer starts walking forward, dragging me by the hand. "To stop talking about this," he says.

Britney didn't drive with us and when we arrive and get inside I spot her dancing in the VIP section, front and center. She's moving her hips slowly, and leaning over the shoulder of Ryan, one of the hosts. His hand is pressed into the small of her back and every once in a while his lips land on her neck. She's got a drink in her hand.

Rainer lets go of me. I look at him and see that he's watching her. "Hey," I say, touching his shoulder. "Dance with me."

I'm thinking about my birthday. How we collided together on the dance floor. How close I felt to him. I want us to get back there. It wasn't that long ago.

"Let's get a drink," he says, like he hasn't heard me.

"Okay."

He leads me over to the VIP section. Immediately, a waitress appears. "Can we get a bottle of Moet and Ketel One?" Rainer asks.

I sit down on a love seat and Rainer sits next to me. It reminds me of the way they had us during the London press junket—I half expect someone to hop underneath the rope and start interviewing us.

I pick at the hem of my dress. I feel uncomfortable being alone with him right now. Earlier, in front of everyone, we were fine. But now that we're alone—sorta—I can feel the whole night swelling around us—Britney and Jordan and the awards. The last few days of silence. Right now, I feel like a stranger in his world. Not his girlfriend.

"She's pretty," I say, watching Britney move.

"Are you jealous?"

I look at him. His eyes are blank, unreadable. I don't know whether he's challenging or consoling me.

"No," I lie. It's not just jealousy, but something else, too. I don't trust her.

"Good."

He turns just as the waitress flies in with our bottles. Crazy. He takes the vodka and pours himself a large glass with a splash of soda. Then he pops the champagne cork.

"Here," he says. He hands me a full glass and I down it in three gulps.

"Easy," he says.

I turn to him. "Why?"

He runs a hand over his chin. "Okay. You're obviously pissed about something." He seems tired, annoyed. I suddenly have the intense desire to not be anywhere near him.

"Look whose talking." I shake my head.

"Is that your way of asking if I'm angry that you sucked face with Jordan in front of the world?"

"Clearly, you are."

"Why should I be?" He's challenging me. "It was just a gimmick, right? An act?"

"Jesus, Rainer, yes. You acted fine about it before."

Rainer takes another swig of his drink. "Sorry if unlike you two I'm not much into making a scene."

I blink at him. I can feel the anger boiling me and I know if I stay, I'll say something I regret. "Forget it," I say. "Forget the whole thing."

I pour myself another glass and then stand up. When he reaches for my arm, I shake him off. "Go talk to Britney," I say. I know it's stupid, and childish, but I feel stupid, and childish. I take off.

I spot Georgina at another banquet bench. She's talking to two girls I don't recognize, but she waves me over.

"Congrats," she says. Wasn't she just devastated over Blake? She doesn't look it. "Did you win, like, every award tonight?"

I hold up my empty glass. "Could you?"

She looks me up and down, impressed. "Slide in." She introduces me as she pours. "This is Christina Hayden and Tailor Coolridge."

"Hi," I say, taking back my glass.

I have no idea who they are, and I don't want to. I don't want to know what network they're on or who their agent is or whether or not they're getting the role of Juliet. Everyone is up for the goddamn role of Juliet. I just want to forget tonight. Rainer's resistance and Britney's judgmental smirk and most of all—Jordan's lips.

"You look like you're having a shit night," Georgina says.

"Could be because I am," I say, downing another glass.

The room starts to spin a little. The edges get softer, worn down, so that it's hard for me to see where things end. Georgina is studying me like she's not sure how to handle the situation.

"My boyfriend is mad at me," I say. "And possibly obsessed with his ex girlfriend. That part is less clear."

Christina snorts. Georgina elbows her. "Should we call Alexis?" she asks.

"Why?" I say. I suppress a hiccup. "She's probably in her sickbed with Jordan."

I squeeze my eyes shut and shake my head. I'm about to totally blow it. *Get it together, Paige.* "Don't listen to me," I say. "I think I'm drunk."

"Think?" Georgina laughs. "Come on," she says. "Let's dance."

Tailor takes me by the elbow and we follow Georgina out to the front of the stage.

I haven't had dinner and as soon as I stand up I feel the champagne in my stomach like liquid gold. It flows through my veins, warming up my blood. It makes everything feel softer. Like the world has less impact.

Georgina is gyrating like the girls onstage and I start to move, too—the champagne making my arms feel long and fluid.

I know people are watching us—let them. Tawny would probably warn me about camera phones, and my dress riding up too short on my thighs, and the clearly alcoholic beverage in my hand—whatever. This isn't her life. It's not Rainer's, either. I don't actually care what anyone says about me. Let them write that I'm a wild child. Maybe I should be.

I'm moving to the music, letting it spin the frustration right out of me. I keep my eyes closed and in the fluttering darkness all I feel is the spreading bliss of numbness. My body has been on hyper-alert for weeks and now it has just stopped caring. The tension flows outward, right along with the music. I'm spinning, lost in the sweat and rhythm and pounding bass of my heartbeat when I feel a hand grabbing at my wrist.

My eyes snap open. Rainer is standing in front of me, a look on his face I've only ever seen him use with his father at the premiere. He's angry. More than angry.

"We're leaving," he says. He has to scream it right into my ear. "Now."

I snatch my hand away. "No," I say. "I'm having fun." I turn back to Georgina, but she's on the other side of the stage, surrounded by people. How did I get this far away on my own?

Rainer pinches the bridge of his nose with this thumb and forefinger. "You're drunk," he says. He looks around to see if anyone is watching us. It makes me even angrier.

"So?"

"I have to get you home," he says, back into my ear, his tone low and dry.

I pull back and away from him. "You have to *get* me home? I'm not your charge, Rainer."

His eyes go wide. "I know that," he says. "You're my girlfriend."

I make a noise somewhere between a cough and a snort.

"You can act out all you want," Rainer says. "But

you're not doing it here. Not where anyone can see. If you want to yell at me at home, fine, but we're going home."

He reaches for me again and this time I take a giant step back, knocking into someone. A few people turn around. I feel the air around us heavy with eyes.

"Stop telling me what to do."

Rainer shakes his head. "PG . . ."

"No," I say. "I'm not going."

He exhales. Lowers his voice. "I can't leave you here, babe."

I'm opening my mouth to protest when Georgina sticks her chin on my shoulder. When did she get here? "I'll look after her, lover boy," she says. "Don't worry."

I see Rainer look from Georgina to me. "I'd rather you come now," he says.

"Stop being so protective," Georgina teases. I feel her arms slip around my middle. "I won't hurt her."

Rainer's eyes find mine. They pierce. "Fine," he says. He takes out his wallet and shoves a bill into my hand. Then he turns and leaves.

"Daddy is pissed," Georgina says, twirling me around. "You're in trouble."

I try to roll my eyes but my lids are so low I'm not sure they're getting anywhere.

"Is he always so protective?"

I nod. But I feel a scraping in my stomach—like some

key rib has come unhinged. I used to love that about Rainer. That used to be the thing that drew us together. That he wanted to make me feel safe and looked out for me in this strange, new world.

I don't see Britney anywhere. I'm aware of the fact that maybe they've left together, but I can't quite grasp what that would mean. I'm too high—on champagne and music and the whirling of Georgina on the dance floor. Forget it. Forget him. Forget it all.

I'm not sure how I find myself on the floor of the lobby bathroom. It seems to happen quickly, but it could be hours later. I'm in a stall, my knees drawn up to my chest. I've thrown up what meager thing we ate—a cupcake? I don't even know.

I take my phone out of my clutch with shaking fingers. It bounces out of my grasp and slides across the stall floor. I grope to take it back. I stare at the screen. I won't call Rainer. I know I should; I know he would come. He might not even give me grief about it. Definitely not until tomorrow, anyway. He'd put me in bed and tell me everything was going to be okay. But I'm not ready to face him. And Alexis is sick. Instead I scroll to J and let my phone dial the one number I know I definitely shouldn't.

He picks up on the first ring.

"Where are you?" he says. Not even hello.

"The lobby of the Roosevelt," I say. "In the bathroom." I squeeze my eyes shut.

"I'm on my way. Stay put."

He shows up quickly. He knocks softly on the stall where I'm crouched down, doing a haphazard job of hiding myself. "Paige?" he says. "It's me."

I come out with my head in my hands. I hear him exhale before I even look at him. "Christ," he says. "What happened?"

I peel my eyes off the floor. "We got in a fight," I say. And then: "Please just take me home."

Jordan looks at the door. I can tell he's nervous. I hadn't thought about how we'd escape once he came. "We have to get through the lobby to go out the back," he says. "They're camped out there and if they see . . ." I watch him take in my crumpled dress, deflated hair, what's probably smeared make up . . . I'm not only drunk, I look drunk. In our world, that's worse.

"Put this on." He takes off his hoodie and drapes it over me. I thread my arms through and zip it to the top.

Jordan pops the hood up. "Come on," he says.

He takes my hand and pulls me out the door. I see a few people look at us when we come out, but I keep my head low. I don't think they recognize us. Jordan tucks his arm around me and we make it outside. When we get there, I exhale against the side door. I press my back against it. The whole world is spinning. I feel like I'm going to faint or throw up. Both, maybe. Jordan pivots and puts his hands on my waist but lower—just on my hips. I feel his fingers dig in. He pins me back, so he's balancing me. "Breathe," he says into my ear. "The car is coming."

I steady my hands on his shoulders. I feel the muscles under there—hard and knotted, like wound rope. My hands start to move over them.

"Paige . . ." Jordan says. His tone is shaky, faulty, but carries a warning.

The car comes around and Jordan helps me inside. It's his pickup. "Crouch down," he tells me before he closes the door. "Just till we're in the clear."

As we pull out of the main entrance I hear the paparazzi scream Jordan's name. I see the flashes—far off and distant. I stay down kneeling in the space between the seat and the glove compartment. My head on my knees.

"You can get up now," Jordan says after a few blocks.

I hoist myself onto the seat. I see his knuckles, white on the steering wheel. I feel humiliated. I stuff my hands in the pockets of Jordan's sweatshirt and lean my head against the window. The glass is cold. I press my cheek flat up to it. My breath makes hazy patterns as we drive.

We don't talk as Jordan winds his truck through the back roads to my house. The house I share with Rainer.

The only car parked in the driveway is the rental. Rainer's

Range Rover is missing. I half expected him to come back here and wait for me, but I guess he went to his mom's.

Jordan unclips his seat belt and turns to me. "Okay," he says.

I take my hands out of the pockets. "Thanks for bringing me back," I say.

"Of course." I see him look at the parked car, dark house.

"He's not home," I say.

Jordan doesn't answer. Instead he pops open his door. "I'll help you inside."

Somewhere between the hotel bathroom and the house I've taken off my shoes, and I hold them in my hand as I stumble towards the entrance. I grope under the mat and find the key. Jordan stands behind me as I push the door open.

It's so quiet here tonight. It has felt like a safe house, like an oasis, but now the quiet seems deafening. It screams to be filled.

I toss my shoes to the side. I turn back to him. "This is it," I say. "This is where we live." Drunken stupidity.

Jordan tilts his head at me. "I know," he says.

I press my hand to my neck. Once again, I think I'm going to be sick.

"Hey," Jordan says. "Come on."

He guides me down the hallway to the bedroom. I stand in the doorway and watch him slip past me to the bed. He tosses the throw pillows on the floor and pulls back the comforter. "There," he says. "That should be sleepable now."

I walk over and kneel on the bed but I can't totally sit up, and I slide down against the pillows, letting my body fall into the soft cotton.

Jordan comes over to me. He pulls the covers up and over, and when his hand is at my chest I reach up and thread my hands through his hair.

"Wait," I say. I remember the morning on Maui. Where I asked him to just sleep with me and he did. But this time he pulls back. He gently plucks my hands from his hair.

"You're drunk," he says.

"Why did you kiss me?" I ask.

"Paige." He sits down next to me. "It was an awards show. We won best kiss."

I shake my head. "You're so angry at me. You try to hide it, but I can tell. Every time you're with me. It's like you hate me. You were so cold on tour. You barely spoke to me on my birthday. Even lunch wasn't the same. And tonight . . ."

I see his chest and rise and not fall. He inhales further. "I don't hate you," he says, but his tone doesn't change.

"Why did you leave tonight?" I ask. "You wouldn't even look at me."

He takes another breath. I can almost feel the effort. "I

don't look at you," he says. He crosses his arms and I keep my fingers curled in my lap, waiting for him to continue. "I don't look at you because when I do, it makes me feel like I can't do my job. I think about the next three years, Paige. About being on Maui with you and acting with you and watching you with him and it makes me want to quit. Leave a job I *love*. Looking at you makes me want to give up."

I feel the tears building. "I'm so sorry, Jordan."

"That's not the point," he says. "You think I don't understand, I *do*. But what am I supposed to do?" He reaches his hand out tentatively, like he's not sure of whether I'll slap him away. And then his hand lands on my cheek. I feel his fingertips there—cool and light—relief. "I can't have you. Worse, I can't even want you."

I stay perfectly still. His thumb runs over my cheek and down to my lips.

"What do you think it's like for me?" I whisper. I can feel my heartbeat everywhere—like a cranked-up stereo system. "I see you with Alexis, too. And I know I don't have a right to care."

Jordan shakes his head, but I push on. "You should move on. I just want you to know . . ." His thumb runs over my bottom lip and they instinctively part. I feel our onstage kiss from earlier.

"Move on," he repeats, almost soundlessly.

"I want you to be happy," I say. I do. I want him to be happy. I realize it like a knife to the heart. Even if it means never being close to him.

"I know," he says. "I want you to be happy, too."

I want to tell him I'm not. I'm not happy. That being away from him is torture. That Rainer isn't here. That I don't know how to help him and I feel alone—really, really alone. But I see the pain in his eyes, and I don't want to make it worse than it already is.

But he's here right now. Really here. It's just the two of us. And it seems ridiculous—absolutely insane—not to reach out and touch him.

So I do. I place my hand on his face. He closes his eyes. "Paige," he says. "Stop."

"I can't," I whisper. My voice is hoarse. I trace his jawline with my fingers. He puts his hands on my shoulders and then runs them down to cup my elbows with his palms. My skin feels like it's being lit on fire. "I miss you," I say. "All the time."

He draws me to him and I think for one brief moment he's going to kiss me, but instead he buries his face in my neck. I feel him groan—his breath hot on my skin. I wrap my arms around him and press my lips to his head.

"I miss you, too," he whispers. He picks his head up. He untangles us slightly, but not all the way. We're still touching. "Look at this," he says. "What if Rainer walked in right now?" His black eyes are hard. "This is his house," he says.

I taste the salt water on my lips. "We're not doing anything wrong." I know we are, but that reality seems light years away.

"Yes," he says, gentler this time. "We are."

"You haven't even . . ."

"Kissed you?" Jordan laughs but it feels cold and mirthless. "This is worse."

I wipe my eyes. "I'm sorry. I didn't call you tonight for this."

"No," Jordan says. "You called me tonight because you were drunk. And maybe you still are and you won't remember this, but I'm not and I will." He takes my hand in his. "I want you all the time, not just when my defenses are down."

"I hate this."

Jordan looks at me. His black eyes have a fleck of gold in them. "You chose him, Paige," he says. "That's all that matters now." He clears his throat. He pulls entirely away from me so we're sitting up, face to face. "That's why I don't think we should see each other," he says. "Not anymore."

I'm so confused that it takes me a moment to register his last words. "What are you saying?"

Jordan shifts on the bed. "We have a good few months before we have to go back and film. I think we should just . . . let things fade."

I sit up and put my hand on his back. I feel him flinch, but he doesn't move away. "Do you really think that will work?"

"I have to try. We've been over this." He gestures with his head to the hallway, and I know he means whatever isn't in this room right now, but is always between us—Rainer.

"Things are such a mess," I say.

I open my mouth to say more, but I'm not sure what else there is. I feel like a character, like August. I thought love triangles only existed in the movies. But here I am, the undeniable third point.

"I'm going to go," Jordan says. "You should sleep."

He stands up and I swing my legs over the bed. The room sways around me and I clutch the edge of the mattress. "So this is it?"

Jordan exhales in the doorway. He puts a hand on the frame and then turns around. My eyes work to find his face in the darkness. "You weren't wrong," he says.

I wait for him to continue.

"About tonight, you weren't wrong. I kissed you because it was the only way I could see being able to be that close to you. It was an opportunity, and I took it. And I'm sorry." And then, right before he disappears, I hear him say. "It won't happen again."

CHAPTER 8

Goddamnit. Goddamnit Goddamnit Goddamnit. I wake up with a pounding headache to the sound of my phone ringing next to my head on the pillow. I open my eyes and try to focus them on the screen. My mother is calling me. My fingers struggle to hit the green button and when they do the room starts twirling itself like it's inside a blender. "Mom?" my voice sounds scratchy in my ears.

"Hey, honey, how are you? We were going to watch the awards last night and then I don't think the cable worked. Is MTV cable, sweetheart? Your father . . ." I close my eyes again.

"Mom, I'll get you a tape, I promise. But I have to call you back."

I run to the bathroom and throw up. And then throw up again.

As I lay on the cold tile I think about last night. Winning best kiss. Jordan taking me home. Fighting with Rainer on the dance floor.

Rainer.

I get up and wash my face. I still feel the house is spinning, but I force myself to focus. I don't let myself think about Jordan, about what it felt like to hold each other here. I can't believe I almost betrayed Rainer like that. In the light of morning I know how right Jordan was. We need to be apart.

I dial Rainer and put the phone to my ear. It rings once and then goes straight to voicemail. Is he screening me? I know he was pissed that I wouldn't leave with him, but I also know Rainer: he's not one to hold on to things like that. I just have to get to him. When we're face to face, I'll say I'm sorry, he'll forgive me, and it will all be okay. I'll apologize for being a drunken mess last night. And an asshole.

I throw on shorts, a hoodie, and Doc Martens, and tuck my hair up into a baseball hat. Then I locate the keys to the rental in the bowl on the kitchen counter.

It's a silver Audi and as soon as I open the doors, my phone buzzes again. I buckle my seatbelt and check the screen, hoping it's him.

Sandy. I groan and pick up. "Sandy, can you give me an

hour please? I had too much champagne last night."

"Paige." Her voice sounds serious. "Where are you?"

"On my way to Rainer's mom's," I say. "Call you in an hour." I hang up, feeling only slightly guilty . . . but I have to prioritize. I type Rainer's home address into the navigation system.

Somewhere, in the recesses of my mind, I see him, arm around Britney, but I let the image retreat back to where it came from. Just because I'm a terrible girlfriend doesn't mean he's doing the same thing.

I drive up through the canyon and down into Beverly Hills, following the navigation's instructions. The streets are so flat and wide here it makes you feel exposed even being in a car. And unlike Santa Monica, no one walks. There isn't a person outside.

I pull up to the Devons' giant, columned home. It reminds me of Cher's house in *Clueless*—all white pillars. Two cars sit in the driveway—but Rainer's black Range Rover is nowhere in sight.

I type in the gate code he gave me and swing around. I've only ever been inside this house and met his mother once, and as I climb the steps and ring the doorbell, my stomach feels like it's been set to boiling. I'm nervous. I wouldn't blame him if he didn't want to see me. What if he's told his mom how horribly I behaved last night? She will hate me, too.

But nobody answers. I ring again. One more. Nothing.

I go back to the car. There is another missed call from Sandy. I dial Rainer's number again. It just rings and rings. Where is he?

I think about his favorite places. Venice, the beach in Santa Monica. Urth Café. I pull out of their gate and then over to the curb. I have no idea where to go. Driving around going in search of Rainer in public places doesn't feel like the best option, but I can't just go home. I need to *do* something.

And then I hear a tap on the window.

I look up to see a man in a black sweater. He's saying something, but I can't understand through the glass. I roll down the window, just halfway, and when I do I see another man behind him, holding a camera. Suddenly the lens is right up against the glass. It happens in three seconds, no more.

I'm blinking, trying to catch up, when he starts firing questions at me. "How long have you been cheating on Rainer? When did it start? Has the affair been going on since you began filming?"

What?

I get it together to roll my window up, but the camera is still there, in my face. I can still hear him yelling questions, but I focus on the car. I shove it into drive and pull out, away from him.

I start driving down Beverly and my phone goes off

113

again. This time it's Alexis. I pick up on the first ring. She'll know what the hell is going on. "Jesus, darling, where are you?" she says.

My voice comes in panicked hiccups. "I fought with Rainer last night. I'm trying to find him . . . And photographers just yelled at me about an affair . . . Going to Urth . . ."

"Do NOT go to Urth!"

"I thought maybe . . ."

"Listen to me," Alexis says, her voice serious. "You are to come directly to my house. Immediately. Do you understand?"

"Have you heard from him?" I ask. "You're making me scared."

"Good," Alexis says. "You should be."

I meet Alexis at her place—a small house in West Hollywood close to The Grove—a shopping center she hates, but still frequents.

She's standing in the open doorway when I pull up. She's wearing a bathrobe over yoga pants and her hair is up in a loose ponytail. I feel a flare of jealousy that she looks this good sick.

"Did anyone see you?" she says. She cranes to look down her street—a tree-lined block that is fairly empty for a Monday in L.A.

"I don't think so?" I follow her as she motions for me to come inside.

She closes the door and exhales dramatically. "Where were you last night?" She's looking at me with a mixture of curiosity and accusation. And suddenly I realize what I've just done: I've come to Jordan's girlfriend for help.

"The MTV Movie Awards," I say. "You know that."

She plucks a tissue out of her pocket and blows. "Of course I know that. I saw you fully embrace your best-kiss win. I mean *after*."

I swallow. "A party at the Roosevelt. Britney threw it. You didn't miss much." Except me getting drunk and trying to make out with your boyfriend.

Alexis shakes her head. She motions for me to follow her through the sunlit living room into her bedroom. Like her, her house is all color and light. Not overly designed but not super casual, either. You get the sense that there are couches for sitting and couches for looking at.

I've never been in her bedroom before and it's more feminine than I would have imagined. Cream and pink silk curtains and a white bedspread with teal and pink stenciled flowers. A black silk nightgown hangs from one of her bedposts and I imagine her slipping it on, Jordan gawking.

"You need to see this," she says. She motions me over to the desk by the window. On it sits a paper-thin laptop. My eyes land on the screen.

Oh. My. God.

The images on the screen are grainy—obviously taken

with a camera phone—but still instantly recognizable. Me and Jordan. Pressed up against the side of the Roosevelt. His hands on my hips and mine on his shoulders. His lips by my ear so it looks like he's kissing my neck. My eyes are closed. *Locked's Love Triangle Leaps Off the Screen.*

No. No. No. No. No. No.

I launch closer to see the website—they're on Perez. Which means they're everywhere. But I already knew that. This is where the paparazzo got his questions. They think I'm cheating on Rainer with Jordan.

"Someone sent in photos to TMZ," Alexis says. "It's not good."

I look at her. Her expression is unreadable.

"I'm so, so sorry," I say. "Nothing happened, I swear." Is that even true? I shake my head. "I'm a shitty friend, and a shitty girlfriend and—oh, God." Rainer has seen these pictures.

I sit down on the edge of her bed. All of a sudden, my legs have given out. My chest is tight, and I can't seem to get enough air.

"Alexis—please, just let me explain."

"This is bad," she says. "I'm not going to lie to you."

I put my head in my hands. Alexis is dating Jordan. She is about to tear my head off, and I deserve nothing less. "I know," I say. "I know. I never meant for—nothing happened, you have to believe me."

Alexis squints at me. "I don't," she says. "But there's an upside to this."

I peel my fingers down. "What?"

Alexis comes and sits next to me. She pulls out another tissue and fluffs her bangs. "I'm not mad at you. Paige, Jordan and I aren't dating."

I look at her. *What?* "You broke up already?"

"We were never dating."

When I don't say anything, she continues. "I don't know how to explain this . . . When the studio saw you and Rainer getting close on set, and then the whole thing happened with Rainer's dad and Brit . . . our reps decided it would be a good idea, if . . ."

"Your relationship with Jordan was a publicity stunt?"

Her face is pale. She nods. "To offset the tension." She's raising her shoulders up, like, *there you go. This happens.*

"Why didn't you say anything?" I ask.

Alexis shakes her head. "Jordan's a friend. We knew it would be a good way to keep any questions from being raised. You know, about the two of you?"

"Oh," I say, picking at my freshly made MTV manicure.

"Which is what you want," Alexis says. "Well, what you wanted."

None of this is what I wanted. I look down at my hands. "Thanks for telling me."

Alexis smiles. "I probably should have made you

guilt-suffer a bit longer." Then she laughs, a much-needed moment of levity, and says: "But did you really think we were actually dating? We have no chemistry!"

"You two are good actors." I pause. "You said it was so hot, and I thought he's always had a thing for you."

Alexis laughs, but it quickly turns into a cough. "No," she says. "He's always been a good friend to me."

"But why lie about it? To me, and to Rainer?" It seems crazy to me that Alexis would hide anything. She's the most self-assured person I know.

"Come on," she says. "You know better than that." Alexis takes her ponytail down and shakes her hair out. It falls in tumbles down her back and I mentally kick myself for not paying more attention, for not being the kind of friend to her she's been trying to be to me. "When you're young, this business is hard. Sometimes faking a relationship gives you more privacy than having the relationship you want."

Her eyes meet mine, and I notice a deep sadness there. I have to look away.

"That's a shitty way to live," I say under my breath.

"Yeah," she says, her voice get quieter. "It's not ideal." Her eyes dart back to the computer screen. Me and Jordan. "I hope you can be honest with me."

"I don't even know what the truth is," I say.

"Well if you don't fill it in soon, those pictures are going to do it for you."

I get up and close the screen. I can't look anymore. "I have to find Rainer."

Alexis rubs her eyes. "So he didn't come home?"

I shake my head. "He wasn't at his mom's house, either. Britney was at the after party last night," I say. "She was with Ryan, but I think—I don't know. I think maybe Rainer left with her."

"No way, he's done with that. He loves you."

"He may not anymore." I blow some air out of my lips and sit back down next to Alexis on the bed. "I can't believe I was so stupid."

Alexis puts a hand on my back. "He'll forgive you," she says. "You just have to make sure that's really what you want."

I glance up at her. "What do you mean?"

"Don't talk him into forgiving you if you're . . ." She clears her throat. "If you're not all in, too." I look at her. Her eyes are big, comforting.

"Alexis, I really screwed up . . ."

She holds out her arms to me and despite her cold I fold into them. I let her hold me. "I know," she says, her hand working to stroke my head. "Find your boyfriend, figure out what you want, make it right."

"You make it sound so easy," I say, dabbing at my eyes with her terrycloth.

"I'm an actress," she says. "That's my job." And then she

plucks me up and gives me a pointed look. "And I'm sorry to be the one to tell you this, darling—But it's yours, too."

I try Rainer ten times from the car. No answer. I have a string of missed calls. Tawny is dialing me every minute, on the minute. I listen to a voicemail from Sandy: "We need to handle this, Paige. Call me back." Her tone is clipped, sharp, rare from her. She means business.

Two from Cassandra, one from my mom, one from my sister. I click off the machine and keep driving. I don't know where to go. I could try the Starbucks Rainer likes at the Beverly Glenn, but being out in public is an idiot's move, and I know it. I saw how quickly Alexis scrolled back up when I tried to read the comments on that Perez piece.

My phone rings again. I look at it, expecting to see Tawny's name on the screen, but instead it's Jordan.

He said he'd stay away, that we needed space, but now the whole world has seen—what? Us together. If there's a way to spin these photos as friendly, I have no idea what it is.

I feel epically, ridiculously horrible about the fact that he's landed in this position. If I hadn't called him last night, drunk and stupid, none of this would have happened. But if I hear his voice, even for a split second, I know I'll fall apart. And I can't afford to do that right now. I hit ignore.

I drive home. I can't think of anything else to do. I'm just about to round the corner and pull into the gate when

I see them—ten parked cars along the side of the road and just as many guys—all decked out in cameras.

They've found us.

My hands leave the wheel and for a split second I think about just gunning it, plowing straight through them. I don't see them as people, now, but insects—small and insidious.

Then they spot me. They start running.

I stop the car right in front of the gate. How am I going to roll down my window to punch in the code?

They descend on me like a summer rainstorm—they drench me in light.

"Paige! When did you start cheating on your boyfriend with his best friend?" "Who do you love?"

"Paige! Just one question!"

"Are you sorry?"

I'm stopped. I can see the house just down the slope, but I have no way to get there. I'm going to die in this car. I'm going to die with these people, these strangers, yelling things about my life that make me feel like the lowest form of pond scum. I sink down in the seat. I put my hands on the wheel. I can feel the panic rising up in my body. It feels like it's going to tear open my ribcage. I don't know whether to laugh or cry. I feel crazy, absolutely unhinged. I get now why you see those pictures of movie stars whacking umbrellas at paparazzi. This could make you snap.

They keep flashing. *Think, Paige. Think.*

I suddenly remember that Rainer gave me a clicker to the gate. I told him it was silly—I could just roll down a window—but he insisted. What did I do with it?

I yank open the glove compartment and let the overstuffed manuals fall to the floor. I find the piece of plastic. Yes. I click it but nothing happens.

Is it broken?

I click it again. Still nothing. Third, fourth time. I whack it against the center console. What is the point in having all this stupid technology if none of it works?

I throw it on the floor but just as I'm about to try to put the car in reverse and back the hell out of here—the gate opens. I half expect the paparazzi to chase me inside, but they don't. They stay on the other side as I pull through and disappear down the hill to the house.

The first thing I see is Rainer. He's standing there, holding an electronic key. He's wearing a blue T-shirt, one of my favorites, and jeans. His hair is ruffled and his eyes are big and red.

I shove the emergency brake on and lock the car behind me.

"They found us," I tell Rainer—half breathless. My heart is racing. Pounding like the first mile of a marathon. "They're all up there. I don't know . . ." but I stop talking. Because he's looking at me in a way that takes all the words right out of my mouth.

"How could you?" he says. I look at him closer. He's been crying.

I shake my head. I feel like I might be sick again.

"Can we go inside?" I say.

He nods. He doesn't want to have this fight outside, either. Not when a long-lens camera could capture something.

I follow him inside. I toss my shoes off and go straight into the living room. I curl up on the couch. "Please come sit with me," I say, not looking up.

"I don't want to sit," he says. "I can't—"

I twist around to look at him. He's pacing the living room, his shirt untucked. He looks like he used to on set sometimes when Wyatt was being particularly difficult. But this is also different. Back then, we were always on the same side. I knew how to make him feel better. What to say, how to touch him. Now he doesn't even want to sit next to me. And who could blame him?

"Please just let me explain," I say. "Those pictures aren't what they look like. I swear to you."

"Fuck that," Rainer says. "They're exactly what they look like."

"No," I say. "They're not. You left last night, and—"

"You WOULDN'T COME HOME WITH ME." Rainer screams. "I left because you made it really clear you didn't want to be around me. And besides—" Rainer waves his hand through the air like he's wiping a blackboard clean. "None of this matters. You weren't with him last night because you were pissed at me. You've been involved with him, whether you'll admit it or not, since the moment you met him. How stupid do you think I am? Honestly, Paige, how stupid are you?"

"Rainer!"

But he's on a roll. "Not too smart if you thought hooking up with Jordan in the middle of the Roosevelt was somehow discreet."

"We didn't hook up at the Roosevelt," I say. "I was drunk and he was helping me get out of there. I promise you, Rainer, those pictures aren't—nothing happened."

"EVERYTHING happened," he says. "You've been lying to me for months. You think you need to hook up with someone to cheat?"

"No," I say. "But I want to be with *you*."

"Do you?" Rainer's eyes flash.

"Yes," I say. "Rainer I chose you. I *live* with you. I love you."

"I don't think you know what you want," Rainer says, pacing. "I think that is our problem here. You say you want me and maybe that's true, but the reality is you want him, too." He looks straight at me. "And I don't think that makes you confused, Paige. I think that makes you selfish."

I gape at him. I'm seeing a side of him I never have before. "I'm sorry, but Rainer—"

"Do you love him?" he asks.

I open my mouth and then close it again. I shake my head. "I don't know."

Rainer puts a thumb to his temple. He closes he eyes. "That's pretty bad," he says.

"I know," I whisper. It feels like all the air has been let out of the room. "I don't know what to say."

Rainer moves suddenly, quickly. "Good," he says. "There isn't anything to say. Go back to Beverly Hills, stay here, I don't care. I'm leaving."

Rainer!" I look at him wildly. "You can't do this. Please, let's just talk about it."

"Don't worry," he says. His words sound tinged with iron. It's like I can taste the metal. "I'll say something discreet—can't have your own co-star trashing your PG rep too." He draws a line in the air from me to him, from his heart to mine. "But it's over. I don't want to be with you. Not anymore."

He turns and leaves then. He doesn't stop when I chase after him, when I start crying, even when I beg. He just walks right to his car, starts it, and pulls out of the driveway without a single glance behind.

Rainer and I have broken up. I am alone.

CHAPTER 9

"Get up."

I peel one eye open to see Alexis standing above me. She's dressed in some see-through white dress and she's got a bandana tied around her head. I shut my eyes against her face and the sun.

"No thanks."

"I'm not getting grass stains on my bottom, Townsen, so stand the hell up."

I reluctantly sit up. I'm out by the pool, at the Bel Air house, the sliding door still open. It feels like I've been lying here for hours, letting my breakup with Rainer play and re-play. I've been doing this for the past day and a half.

I made the mistake when he left of going online. I read everything. There isn't a single gossip column, newspaper or trade that isn't running this story with varying degrees of hysterical exaggeration. In one of them, I'm pregnant with Jordan's baby.

In a matter of minutes I became public enemy number one. I cheated on Hollywood's reigning golden boy. I broke up Raige. People are pissed, devastated, and yet some are elated. There are whole factions of fans (Team Ed) who have been gunning for me to be with Jordan all along. The headlines are horrifying—so ridiculous and over the top they make me feel like I'm trapped in a nightmare.

Raige Crashes to an End
Paige Betrays Her Noah
Paidan Takes the Lead

The worst part, though, was coming clean to my mom.

Once I stopped sobbing I called her. She picked up the phone immediately and as soon as I heard her voice, I lost it again. Completely broke down. I was going to try to be strong—I'd had a little speech I had practiced about how the press makes up stories and you can't believe a word of it . . . it's what I told Cassandra (not that she bought it). But the moment I heard my mom's voice on the other end of the line, I knew I had to tell her the truth.

I told her everything. Things I hadn't told Cassandra or even, probably, admitted to myself. She just listened. She didn't say anything, not a word. When I was finished and had stopped crying, she took a breath.

"Come home, honey," she said.

Here's a little secret I'll tell you about being famous. People talk about temptation all the time. The money. Access to drugs. Booze. Parties. They talk about fad diets and binging in the bathroom and eating one meal worth my parent's entire mortgage.

But the greatest temptation you'll ever feel when you're famous is to just give up and go home. To go back to where you came from and send the spotlight reeling towards someone else.

"Just get on a plane, Paige."

"Mom . . ." I wiped my tears away.

"That's right," my mom said gently. "We'll deal with this together. You just have to get out of there."

"It's not that easy," I said. "It would follow me there. And I'm under contract."

"We can figure all that out. Your life in Portland—"

My life in Portland. Trinkets N Things. Joanna and Annabelle taking over every room in the house.

"—was a good life, Paige. People will forget eventually. You could go to college." She sounded almost cheerful.

"Not act?" I said, the thought making my chest seize up. "You know I can't do that." The truth was, I didn't even know how I'd get to the airport to get home, let alone give up my life here.

"I think you don't know what you can do," my mother

said. It went on this way for another half hour. She even put my sister on, who told me if I was home I could help with the wedding. We could have sister-bonding time. It actually sounded appealing, which is how I knew I had officially gone crazy.

Alexis taps my leg with her stiletto, bringing me back to the present. I groan and drop my head onto my knees. "Not now," I say.

Alexis crouches down next to me. "I called you a hundred times," she says. "I'm sorry, drastic times, drastic measures."

"Shouldn't you be giving interviews about how much I suck? I slept with your boyfriend."

Alexis throws her head back. "There is not one single part of that sentence that is true." Her eyes fixate on me. "Is there?"

I groan. "What does it even matter? Everyone is deciding the truth for me anyway."

"So that's it?"

"What's what?"

"You're just going to give up, call it quits, spend the rest of your life on this mediocre lawn."

"This is more lawn than you have," I mutter.

Alexis yanks me up by the elbow. She's got some serious strength. "You need help," she says.

"Send a therapist."

"No, I mean, you need someone to tell you what to do."
I rub my eyes. "Are you going to do that?"

Sandy has called. I told her to be there for Rainer. Tawny came by. I immediately kicked her out. They all want me to make statements: Tawny saying how sorry I am to have betrayed Rainer, whom I love, and Sandy wants a joint statement with Rainer and I denying any wrongdoing on my part. I don't know what to do. "You need to set the record straight for your fans," Tawny told me.

What they're all failing to realize is that I don't know what the record *is*. How can I set it straight? I didn't sleep with Jordan, but I did betray Rainer. He broke up with me. He knows. Why does the world need to?

"You shouldn't even be here," I mutter as Alexis leads me inside. "I'm the worst. I probably broke your fake heart. Why would you come visit me?"

Alexis raises her eyebrows at me. "My heart is real, thank you very much. It just was never Jordan's."

"I'm sorry," I say. "That's not what I mean."

Alexis rolls her eyes. "Relax, I know."

I desperately want to ask Alexis if she's heard from Jordan and how he is, *where* he is, but I'm not sure I'm prepared to know. I left an apology on his voicemail, but I haven't heard back from him. Maybe he was right—maybe we shouldn't speak anymore.

"Georgina has offered Malibu to us while she's in

Atlanta. She won't be back until next month."

"Have you seen the army at my gate?" I ask her. "How do you propose we *get* to Malibu?"

"Oh please," she says, eyeing me up and down. "You think this is my first human heist?"

An hour later I'm in the back of Alexis's Porsche Cayenne, covered in a quilt. We've packed up essentials—clothes, toiletries, laptops, cell phone, and made it out of the gates. I hear the shouts and screams. Luckily I can't make most of the specifics out.

We pull out of Bel Air and I sit back up as we turn onto Sunset and make our way across to Santa Monica and then the PCH. I watch the ocean as we pass. I wonder what would happen if I just forced my way out of the car right now and ran straight in. Would someone catch me?

"A few things," Alexis says, glancing in the rearview at me. "First things first: I'm going to get you through this, but you need to call Sandy back, and you need to set a meeting with your agent." Alexis shakes her head at me. "No excuses. This will blow over, but it's big, and you need to talk to them about how you're going to rehab your image. You need to be smart, Paige."

I cross my arms. "Fine," I say.

"And drop the attitude, darling," she says. "No one

likes a grump. Especially when she's trying to recover from a very public scandal."

"Anything else?"

Alexis's eyes flash in the mirror as she makes a left into the Colony. "No laying out without me," she says. "If we get tan, we get tan together."

She parks and I grab my duffle out of the back. I follow her up the stone steps, but the front door is already open. For a moment I have a flash of panic—the paparazzi have made it inside the colony. They're here. They found us already. But then I see him standing in the doorway. I am flooded with relief and then immediately dread—he doesn't look happy.

"Oh yeah, one last thing," Alexis says, passing him and disappearing into the house. "Listen to him."

I look at Wyatt, his arms crossed and his black jeans and Ramones T-shirt combo offsetting his wild, curly head of hair. He's wearing a look I've seen a lot before. He's not happy.

"I go away for one fucking month and this is what happens?"

I hike my bag up farther, but I don't take a step towards him.

"Well come on," he says when I don't move. "I can't yell at you until I've hugged you."

And then Wyatt Lippman, our infamously tempera-mental director, is making his way towards me. He takes off my bag, puts it down on the ground. It feels like he takes a lot more than my duffle. And then he puts his hands on my shoulders. I lean into him, stiff, but then he pats my back and I put my head on his shoulder. The tears come fast and furious. Everything from today, yesterday. The breakup, the tabloid headlines, those pictures—capturing the most confusing, personal moment and making it so harshly public—all come out in Wyatt's comforting embrace.

"Now you give me emotion," he says, chuckling.

Wyatt doesn't let me off easy, but I don't expect him to. He was the one who first warned me about dating Rainer. He didn't like it.

"I expected more," he says.

"I know."

"You're not like those other girls. Running around drunk with no pants on. Come on, PG, don't let me be wrong about you."

"I'm not. It was one stupid moment. Rainer and I got in a fight and he . . ."

Wyatt sits on a stool at Georgina's counter, a glass of water in front of him. Like in Hawaii, he looks unbelievably uncomfortable at the beach. It fills me with something close to comfort. "Jordan," he says.

I see Alexis through the sliding glass doors. She's outside, giving us space, but I know she's eavesdropping. I wonder if she can hear anything with the ocean behind her.

I put my elbows on the counter and thread my hands around my water glass. "Have you spoken to him?" I ask.

Wyatt shakes his head. "PG, listen to me. It doesn't matter. You gotta let this go. This is not a love triangle, okay? This is not fiction; this is real life. You have to put this personal bullshit—all of it—behind you. You have a job, a real one. You need to go back to Maui ready to work."

"I can't even think about that."

"Well you're gonna have to," Wyatt says. "You know I don't like to get personal," he says, but his eyes have softened. "But I am telling you to stop with the both of them. Date someone from home. Date someone you met at the dog park—"

"I don't have a dog."

Wyatt waves his hand in the air like *whatever*.

"So get one. Just stop keeping company with your co-stars," he finishes. "What you need to worry about now is gaining back your fans' trust."

I shake my head. "How?" I say.

Wyatt laughs. He clocks my shoulder. "PG," he says. "You're a pretty girl and a great actress, but sometimes you can be really thick."

"A great actress? Now I know you're lying."

"Nah," he says. "That one is all truth." Wyatt looks at me. His curly hair looks like it has grown six inches outwards in this salt air while we've been talking.

"I don't want to do this without you," I say. "Are you really not coming back?"

Wyatt chucks me under the chin softly. "I'm here now," he says. "Let's talk about what you need to do."

Wyatt lays out rules. No partying, no shopping, no staged paparazzi pics with "the crew." No dating movie stars. No drinking. Get a non-*Locked* job. When he leaves, I pull open my laptop. Alexis is outside, talking on the phone. I see her hands gesturing wildly.

Hour by hour, the story continues to spread. It's posted even more places than it was this morning. It feels like the entire internet is devoted to hating me. There are real world problems, there is NEWS, but none of that is front and center. It's just me, my body pressed against the side door of a hotel, and Jordan leaning over me.

Fans Rage at Raige

They don't know what they're talking about. They're wrong. I want to throw my computer across the room. I want to make my own YouTube video, give an interview, anything to have a voice in this deafening chorus of cries. The whole world is a bully and I can't defend myself. I can just go into the bathroom, balance my lunch tray on my lap, and cry.

This is what I've been afraid of, and it's just as bad as I thought it would be.

And then I see a headline: "EXCLUSIVE: Close Source Speaks Out About Paige and Jordan's Affair."

My blood turns to ice in my veins.

I click on the link with shaky fingers.

A source close to Paige Townsen, a young woman who asked to remain anonymous, spoke exclusively to Fansugar regarding the Paige/Jordan affair. "I know Paige had feelings for Jordan for a long time. Since he first got to set. They hooked up once or twice when Rainer was away. She's pretty fickle. She used to date a guy in Portland who was a friend, but she ditched him for Rainer the second she got to Maui."

I feel my heartbeat slow to a stop in my chest. No one knew about Jake. No one but my family, and Cassandra.

"It won't last with Jordan and it won't last with Rainer. Paige would never admit this, but she's not reliable in love. She's in over her head."

I think about the two times Cassandra has been out here. At the premiere I told her everything about Jordan. How I'd fallen for him on Maui and how confused I was. But there's no way she'd do this. I know Alexis and Georgina warned me about old friends, but they don't know Cassandra like I do. Cassandra is *Cassandra*.

But how did they find out? Who sold me out? Is it possible I told Alexis or Georgina that Jake and I used to date? Would they do this?

I think about Alexis, how kind she has been. And Georgina offering us her home to hide out. I have no idea.

The only conclusion I can come to is that you can't trust anyone, not a single soul. Not even your best friends.

I close the laptop. I feel lightheaded, and nauseous. I blink a few times and see Alexis at the door, a pitcher of lemonade in her hands.

She comes towards me, a concerned look on her face. "Everything okay?" she asks.

"No," I say. "It's not."

The breakup with Rainer is brutal—it feels like shards of glass swimming around in my chest cavity. But now I don't even know who I can talk to. I have no idea who I can trust. And that, that isolation, that's like a puncture straight to the heart.

Alexis pulls a glass down and hands me a cup. Then she puts her arm around me. She's so much taller that I just lean into her side. "You have to tune it out and turn it off," she says. "It's the only way you'll survive."

"I guess so," I say. Add it to the list of things I didn't know about this life . . . I didn't know getting to do what I love would mean giving up the freedom to be who I am. I didn't know that the world would decide that for me. I didn't know I'd have to hold things so close to my chest they wouldn't even have the space to breathe.

CHAPTER 10

"It's *The Little Mermaid*, but for teens. You would play the girl who is torn between her sea-man love, and a human."

I look at Sandy. We've been in my agent, Amanda's, office for forty-five minutes and all I've heard are ideas for other YA franchises. Angels incarnated as mean girls, a princess who turns out to be an alien and takes over the nation. When Wyatt told me to get a job, I don't think this is what he meant. I half expect them to start pitching me a love triangle about gnomes in outer space.

Finally I ask it: "What are we really doing here?"

Sandy dragged me out of bed this morning. For the past week I haven't left Georgina's. Alexis put a ban on the computer and she has given me limited control over my cell phone, too.

Everyone keeps telling me it's going to blow over, but no one will say when. Every day there are new stories. Rainer is back together with Britney. Jordan and Alexis broke up. We went to Maui to sort everything out. We've all quit the franchise. The whole thing is a publicity stunt.

Publicity stunt. Right. Because this press is so glowing and radiant.

I've had a headache for days. Something is chewing away at the vertebrae of my neck. Maybe I have meningitis.

Sandy agreed with Alexis—it's better for me to lie low. Rainer is following suit, too. He hasn't made any statements, and neither have I. "Silence is golden," Sandy keeps saying. "Any energy is going to make it bigger."

She has remained firmly on my side, *and* Rainer's. I don't pretend it is any small feat.

"Just make me one promise," she told me. "Do not, under any circumstances, see Jordan Wilder."

I've kept it.

Sandy gives Amanda a raised eyebrow. Amanda leans forward. She's in her thirties, with jet-black hair that is always pulled back in an expertly styled bun. She wears glasses and dress suits and generally has a scarf tied around her neck. She's the best in the business, and she terrifies me.

"I know you're aware this scandal—" Sandy clears her throat, but Amanda continues. "Hasn't been good for your image."

"No way," I deadpan.

"We're holding tight to your Lancome deal, but it hasn't been easy."

"Are they pulling their offer?"

Amanda threads her hands together. "They want to. But we won't let them. The point is that right now your image is in the toilet."

"What she means to say is—" Sandy interjects.

"What she means to say is exactly that," I finish for her.

Amanda nods. "Sorry, but it's true. We'll be able to rehab, but the stuff you want isn't available right now. What *is* available are these franchises. You're still killing it at the box office."

Locked is having a second life. Box office numbers haven't been this good since opening weekend. Everyone wants to see the love triangle come to life on the big screen.

"Have you heard any more about *Closer to Heaven*?" I ask.

Sandy and Amanda exchange a glance. "I think we want to move in a different direction," Amanda says, speaking slowly. "*Closer to Heaven* might not be the right role to launch you post *Locked*."

"They don't even want to consider me anymore," I whisper. What little opportunity I had for that part went away the second I put my hands on Jordan.

Sandy puts her hand on my knee. "It's not that," Sandy

says. "It's just that they were already concerned about you being thought of as the *Locked* girl. You're at maximum exposure now."

"But you won't always be," Amanda offers. "Not in this way. Not if we make the right moves now."

Amanda types something into her computer, then stops and looks at us. "Now more than ever I want us all to be on the same page about The Career." The Career. She uses the term "the career" constantly. Never "mine," always "the."

"I'm not sure we are," I say.

Both Sandy and Amanda stare at me.

"I love *Locked* and that's just the point—I want to do projects that inspire me. *There* did. *Closer to Heaven* does. This Mermaid thing doesn't."

Amanda opens her mouth to counter, but I keep talking. "Neither does Sunset Rivals or that one you pitched me about Salem Witches reincarnated. I don't want to do any of that. Nothing with a green screen. I want to do a real, human story. I want to *act*."

"Sweetheart," Amanda says, her tone clipped. "You'll be *acting* in all of these."

Sandy holds her hand up. "We're going in circles," she says. "We said we weren't going to leave this office until we came up with next steps."

Amanda switches tactics. "Listen, I get it, believe me. When Jennifer finished *Trident* the only thing she wanted to do was some small-budget indie. There are incredible scripts out there but you know where the REALLY amazing scripts end up? Studios. You want the version of *Closer to Heaven* that has some traction behind it. You think all you need is a great script and a director with some vision but really what you need is belief and support and MONEY."

Sandy nods. "She's right. I hate to say it. A lot of these movies turn out terrible, or worse, don't even get released."

"Exactly," Amanda says. "And we can't have your first role post scandal be something two thousand people in an art theater see." She stands up and comes around the front of her desk. "We're on the same side. We want you to do projects you love. That's the point of this whole thing. But we also want you to have a long career. Let's not forget that *Locked* is one movie."

Sandy puts her hand on my shoulder. "It has been a rough week, right?"

"I'm not trying to get a sympathy vote," I say. "I'm not . . ."

"We're not dwelling," Amanda says, holding up her hand. "We will get through this. We just want to know our options right now. And our options are the things I've pitched you. You're in a rocky moment, okay, but that doesn't mean you're not still the hottest young actress in Hollywood. Remember, what you do now matters. For better or worse, everyone is watching."

Everyone is watching.

I think about the photographers that are parked outside the Colony daily. I heard a neighbor talking about the disturbance next door. I feel bad. Terrible, actually. No one else asked for this. It's bad enough that I can't even go to Starbucks or to the grocery store or on a run, but now strangers are being harassed in and out of their homes. All because of me.

"I've had my life taken away," I say. "That's the thing I don't think you realize. The work is the ONLY thing that's good about this. I can't—" My voice breaks, but I push through. I've cried too much over this already. "I can't give that up, too."

"Understood." Sandy cocks her head in Amanda's direction. *We're done.*

"We'll get the *Closer to Heaven* meeting," Amanda says. "Even if I have to trade favors. But I'm going to keep sending scripts, and you're going to keep reading them. I want you in the press for what you're doing, not who—"

"I get it," I say. I don't need that sentence finished.

Amanda holds the door to her office open for us. The first thing I want to do is call Rainer, tell him about this meeting and ask his advice. It's so strange that he's not here, that I can't go to him for help. Maybe it's because of this that I stop Sandy as we get in the elevator. "How is he?"

She makes a fuss of re-perching her sunglasses on top of her head. "Okay," she says. "The family stuff is dying down, a bit."

It's true. Every tabloid story has replaced Greg's affair with mine.

I want to ask her the next question, but I don't. I don't get to know.

Sandy puts a hand on my shoulder. "Yes," she says. "He misses you. He won't admit it to me, but I can tell. I've known the kid forever."

I choke back words. I miss him, too. Palpably. Sometimes I lie awake and hear the ocean and I think we're back on Maui. That it's me and Rainer on that movie set, falling for each other all over again.

I think about a headline I saw discarded in Amanda's office. *Locked Out of Love*. No kidding.

"Where are you off to?" she asks.

Oh, you know. Lunch at The Chateau, drinks on Melrose, a walk in Santa Monica. "Malibu," I say. Like I have a choice.

Sandy nods. "Listen, we have to talk about Tokyo."

I pause. The elevator doors close on us. "What?"

She squints at me. "Japan? Comiket? Don't tell me you've forgotten."

"Damnit." The studio is sending me, Jordan and Rainer to the biggest comic-book conference in the world. Three days, the three of us. I totally spaced on it. "When?"

Sandy pulls out her phone. "Monday."

"That's three days from now!"

She nods. "The convention was contracted a long time ago, but if you ask me it might be a good time to show the world you all can still get along." Sandy gives me a pointed look.

"Can we?"

"I know this is less than ideal," she says. "But I think we should look at it as an opportunity."

"Things can't really get a whole lot worse," I say.

Sandy eyes me as the elevator doors open, delivering us to the parking garage. "Honey," she says. "You're on house arrest at a Malibu mansion. Trust me, things could get a LOT worse."

Sandy is not entirely wrong. Three days later, we're leaving for Tokyo, and nothing is right between us. I still haven't spoken to Jordan or Rainer. And Alexis isn't coming to Japan.

They are, however, sending Jessica as our wrangler. She shows up in a town car Monday morning, her long, blonde hair pulled up into an effortless ponytail. She's wearing jeans and a gray sweatshirt with a pink heart on the front. "Hey, PG," she says. "What can I help you with?"

Alexis is sitting at the counter, hunched over some

green tea. It's six AM. She's going to go work out, and I'm going to get on a plane with Jordan and Rainer and fly across the world. They're sending us private—perhaps in a bid for us to work it out away from prying eyes before we land. Good luck.

Despite the early hour, Jessica is as perky as ever. I remember her positive attitude at many five AM call times on Maui. "How did you get dragged into this?" I ask her.

She pops up the handle of my suitcase. "Wyatt is busy working," Jessica says. "They asked if I could fill in. I said of course."

"I think I should come," Alexis says. "I feel weird about you being alone with them."

Jessica averts her eyes. I know she's trying to give us privacy.

"I'll be fine," I say. It's the same thing I told her last night. And the night before. She's been worried about me, about what will happen when I'm on the other side of the world with both of them. Since I moved in here she's been watching me like a bomb about to detonate.

"Darling," she told me. "Your restraint doesn't seem to be in full effect lately."

I know Alexis has spoken to Jordan, but she doesn't talk about it with me, and out of respect, I haven't asked. Maybe her anxiety comes from things *he's* said. Maybe he wants her there.

"We should go," Jessica says. I see the same look on her face that she would wear every time she came into hair and makeup. I'd be in Lillianna's chair, and we'd be behind schedule. It was Jessica's job to get us to set. She had this great way of keeping us moving while maintaining a calm, cool atmosphere. You never saw Jessica sweat.

I hold my arms open to Alexis. She gives me a big hug. "Call me if you need me," she says.

"I will."

"You're wonderful," she whispers. "Just as you are. Remember that."

"Thanks. You should go out while I'm gone. Have some fun. I've been keeping you here too much."

Alexis smiles. "This forced hibernation has been great for my mystery factor, but now that you mention it, I have been kind of cooped up . . ."

I kiss her cheek. "Just don't get photographed making out in public."

Alexis laughs. "Amateur move," she says.

Jessica gives Alexis a little wave as we close the door. She hands my bag to the driver and gets in the front seat, next to him. I hope we can stop for coffee. I let the driver hold the door open for me, and then I'm sliding into the backseat, and we're off.

CHAPTER 11

We've been on planes before, the three of us. On our first promotional tour of *Locked*, when I was with Rainer. Even though it's only been a month, everything is different. Rainer and I aren't together, and Jordan and I aren't, either, and no one is friends, or even pretending to be. No one is speaking.

I sit alone. Jessica takes out a game of Scattegories and she and Rainer play. Jordan sits somewhere near the back. I see him only briefly when we board, and then he disappears out of sight. I know I can't follow him, so I settle somewhere in the middle, by the window, away from them both.

The tension on the plane is tight, palpable. I close my eyes to see if it's safer there. I'm surprised at how quickly I fall asleep.

I wake up intermittently, and when I do everyone else is asleep. Jessica and Rainer are curled up together. I think they fell asleep playing Connect Four. I find some water and down it. I read for a little while, but I'm distracted, anxious, and still groggy. After a few hours I give up and pass back out. When I wake up this time, it's to a rocky landing. We're met at the gate by security. Five guys in all black lead us into a waiting town car. But word must have gotten out that we're here, because even at the private airport, people are waiting.

I've heard the fandom in Asia in intense, but nothing prepares me for the hysteria we're met with as we make our way to the cars. People claw and cry. They yell and scream and snap photos. It's crazy, insane. Instinctively I look for Rainer, but he's already moving ahead of me, lost in between two bodyguards. I have to brave this one on my own.

The three of us pose for pictures outside and sign autographs. Rainer doesn't hold tightly to my hand. He doesn't whisper in my ear that it's only going to be three minutes. He doesn't even look at me.

We go straight to the hotel. No one speaks in the car except for Jessica and Rainer. We check in and I'm not surprised to find that my room is right next to Rainer's. I think they're used to doing it from the last tour, and maybe no one alerted the people who make these reservations to the fact that we're no longer together.

We disappear quickly into our separate rooms. I think about how different this is from last time. Last time we'd open them up. One would become a dressing room and the other a bedroom. We'd have this enormous, sprawling double suite, all to ourselves.

But now it's just me. The room is beautiful. All colors—turquoise and fuchsia and sea foam green. It looks like being inside a kaleidoscope and I feel the pull to call Cassandra like gravity. Cassandra loves color so much; she's constantly making up her own. I see some pumpkin pie pillows and pick up the phone. One nice thing about being a celebrity? You don't have to worry about international rates.

"Hey, stranger," she says. "Where in the world are you?"

"Tokyo," I say.

"No way! How are you? Are the boys there with you? What is going on? Tell me everything!"

I know Cassandra wasn't the leak, she would never do that, but I still feel myself begin to lie. To my best friend. "They're fine," I say. "We're good."

"That's such a relief," she says. "Because the stories are . . ."

"Just stories," I say. "Everything is okay."

"Okay," Cassandra says. Her voice has gotten quieter. I can almost hear her picking her nails. "How is everything else?"

"Good," I say. I know she registers the false cheerfulness in my tone.

"Tokyo, huh?" she says.

"Yeah, crazy."

"Well, have fun, I guess."

"Thanks," I say.

We hang up and I feel worse than I did when I called. Stupid. I push it out of my head. We have two hours until we have to go to the convention center, and I need to shower. Someone for hair and makeup will be here any minute. But I feel like I'm still sleep-adjacent. I haven't yet recovered from the flight and the weirdness of being across the world with the two of them. I face-plant into the bed. Just five minutes, and then I'll get up.

A knock at the door jolts me upright. I wipe the drool off my face and glance at the clock—I've been out for thirty minutes. I get up and shuffle to the door, expecting to see hair and makeup with their bags of goodies, but instead it's just Jessica. Freshly showered, cell phone in hand.

I wipe my eyes. "Am I late?" I say.

Jessica laughs. "I know I'm not always the most

welcome sight but geez, Paige. I was just coming to see if you needed anything."

I shake my head. "I'm all good."

"Cool. Hair and makeup are on their way up." She eyes me. "You may want to hop in the shower."

"See?" I say. "Late."

Jessica holds up her hands. "It was just a suggestion!"

She turns to leave when I stop her. "Hey," I say. "Could you do me a favor?"

"Of course," Jessica says.

"Could you keep Rainer company?"

She looks at her phone. I see her bite her bottom lip. I always forget she's twenty-three. She seems so young sometimes, so sweet and naïve.

"I . . ."

I shake my head. "I know he's going through a lot right now, and Sandy isn't here. And . . ." I let my voice trail off. "He likes you," I say. "I saw you hanging out on the plane. You can get through to him in a way I just . . . I can't right now. It would mean a lot to me."

Jessica nods. "Of course," she says. "Maybe he wants to come with me to make sure the Evian bottles are packed in the van. Non-stop drama and intrigue." She laughs. So do I.

"I think a little non-drama would be good for him," I say.

"A little non-drama would be good for you all," Jessica says.

As Sandy told me, Comiket is the world's largest comic-book market that is held twice a year here in Toyko. Over half a million people come from all over to buy rare editions of their favorite comics. It's Asia's answer to Comic Con . . . just much, much bigger.

Sandy also told me that up until recently Hollywood hasn't played much of a role in Comiket, but this year they're sending us. We're giving away signed copies of the *Locked* trilogy—personalized by the author, Parker Witter, herself (a rare thing, given the fact that she's somewhat of a recluse)—and signing headshots, magazines, and a line of graphic novels the studio has made based on the books.

There are many strange things about being in a movie this large. People you don't know recognizing you, fan fiction about your real life appearing on the internet, never really trusting that no one is watching—but one of the strangest has to be the merchandise. There are tiny dolls of Rainer, Jordan and I. Rainer's has his dimples, mine has my red hair, Jordan's even has his scar.

Comiket is held at Tokyo Big Sight—a convention center, the largest here. There are droves and droves of people lining the streets as we pull through. Alexis has told me Comic Con is crazy, but I'm not sure anything could compare to this. We're in a black limo, windows fully tinted. I have no doubt that if we were seen right now we'd be mauled to death in a matter of seconds.

Rainer is sitting next to me, his fingertips trailing on the seat and for a moment I want to brush against them, hold them in my hand. It's tense in the car, but with this many people, and this much energy and noise—there isn't room for outward animosity. Not between any of us.

"Amazing," Rainer says to no one in particular.

Jessica starts laughing. "That's not the word I would use."

"What would you use?" Rainer asks.

"Scary."

I look at Jessica. She's in her same jeans/T-shirt combo. They sent me over here with all kinds of crazy outfits. I'm right now wearing leather pants and a red silk blouse.

I miss the days of being Jessica. Where not everything I said, wore, did was scrutinized with more precision than a rocket launch.

"Fear won't help us much," Rainer says, not taking his eyes off the crowds. Jordan stays silent.

They get us inside by some miracle—I don't know how they do it. But Toyko is like a toy city—a maze of lights and characters and colors.

We get into the basement and are immediately joined by the guys who met us at the airport—except this time they've brought their friends. There must be ten security guards, but I can't be sure, because they seem to multiply every time I try to count. Which I guess is good. We should be surrounded here.

We're set up on a stage and as we're led up the elevator and down the corridor I hear the people. They're not chanting our names, but the mere buzz of it—the energy of their anticipation—has a volume all its own.

Rainer is making his usual, good-natured banter. It's directed at Jessica now. Jordan is still silent. I can feel the tension in his body. It seems to come off of him in waves.

The bodyguards are blocking us even from one another, but I find his eyes. I want more than anything to reach out and hold his hand.

But instead I touch my fingers to the cowry shell charm on my chest. I've taken off the ring Rainer gave me, but I haven't removed the necklace, not even to shower. It's my mark of protection. It's Rainer's stand-in.

Jessica and the publicist look back at me. "You guys ready?"

Jordan makes an indeterminate sound, but they don't wait for an answer. They open the doors and the screams are massive—a tidal wave of bodies and sound.

It's hot in there, too. Stifling. Everyone crammed on each other every which way— I start to sweat immediately. Beads cling to my forehead. Who decided on these leather pants? I feel like they're melted onto my skin.

We're seated on stage. The three of us in a row. Me in the middle. Magazine covers and our own action figures are splayed out all around us. Jessica is saying something to me, but I can't hear her above the noise. She comes around to my chair, gets close in my ear. "Can you do pictures?"

I nod, and for a moment I look at Jordan next to me. His eyes are wide—a look I recognize well. He's scared. It hits me like a sucker punch straight to the chest. I see myself in his dilated pupils. The fear, the paranoia, the terror.

His black eyes look into mine and I'm met with such intensity it makes me want to weep. But instead of being pulled under with him, something else happens. I feel an urge to protect him. The tenderness I feel overrides everything else. I want to make this better. Something rises up in me, some core of solid steel. I have been so used to being the one looking to Rainer in these circumstances, giving into my fear—every incarnation of it—that I haven't stopped to think about *them*. Rainer and Jordan. Alexis always stayed with Jordan at premieres and I know it was because of this. She acted for him the way Rainer did for me.

I think about that signing on Maui. How it was just Jordan and I—our first experience with fans. He left me in the car and at the time I was so angry. I couldn't understand his distance, that he hadn't stood by me in those first few moments with fans, but now I realize he couldn't have done it any differently. He couldn't look out for me. He was too busy trying to keep himself afloat.

I search under the table for his hand. I find his fingertips. They're cold as ice. I hold them between my palm. I lean over to him. I whisper into his ear, even though I know I shouldn't, even though I know there are cameras everywhere. "Three minutes," I tell him. "It's only scary for three minutes."

Jordan's face softens, just slightly. I bet he's heard it before. I bet Rainer told him years ago, back when they were friends. And that feels right, somehow. I think about Rainer and I making those promises to each other on the cliffs of Maui—the moment I've called up so many times. Whatever's coming, I'll be here. But now I understand it should have been bigger than that, than the two of us. It's not about just Rainer and I: it's about all three of us. We're *all* in this together.

I keep Jordan's hand in mine under the table until the first person comes up for an autograph.

It feels good to hold my own. The least I can do for all of us, and the fans—is try. And the truth is that once it's one on one—thanks to the well-managed line— greeting fans isn't so scary. Some people cry. Some people get hysterical. One incredibly overwhelmed girl actually faints. But a lot of people are just *happy*. Happy to see us, happy to talk about their favorite book, or movie. And the fact that we've contributed to that happiness, even a little bit, seems to momentarily smooth over the personal drama we're going through. It hovers above Paige, Rainer and Jordan. It's bigger than us. It's the sum of us and so much more. To be a part of something that will outlast us—that will outlast whatever happens *between* us. Together we've made something that will prevail, and for an hour, I let that be our legacy.

After the signing we go back to the hotel. When we get to the lobby, we start to split off for our rooms, but Jessica stops us.

"I made reservations at three different restaurants," she says. Her tone is hopeful, bright. Her eyes look from me to Rainer to Jordan. "One even has a view of Mt. Fuji. Supposed to be the best sashimi in the city . . ."

"Sounds great," Rainer says. "I definitely want to see what this city has to offer."

"Thanks, Jess," Jordan says. "But I'm gonna pass. I'm pretty beat."

"Are you sure?" Jessica asks.

Rainer clears his throat. "I'm gonna go power nap," he says, ignoring Jordan's opt out. "Then we're getting involved in this foreign land. I've been spending way too much time inside lately." He slings an arm over Jessica. It feels intentional, like he's punishing me. For a moment

I'm struck by this gnawing jealousy, remembering that it used to be me there with him. "Meet you down here in an hour?" he says to her.

Jessica shimmies out from under him. "Sounds good."

Rainer strides towards the elevators and Jessica angles towards me. "You're coming, right?"

I will myself not to look at Jordan. I keep my eyes trained on Jessica. "That trip killed me," I say. "Tomorrow night?"

"Absolutely!" Jessica says brightly. "I have your copy of tomorrow's schedule in the room," she says. "Want to come up with me?"

I look back at Jordan, but he's already crossing the lobby to the other set of elevators. "Sure."

CHAPTER 12

An hour later I find myself in the lobby of our hotel waiting for a new room key when Rainer comes down. They had to switch me to another floor, something about a broken radiator, I didn't really understand.

He sees me and stops. We both just stand there, not sure of what to do.

"Hey," I say. "Where's Jessica?"

Rainer shrugs. "Late."

I nod. Okay.

I notice he's wearing my favorite button down—a purple and white striped shirt that he bought to wear on one of our first proper dates in L.A. I wonder if he put it on with intention. If he remembers how I threaded my fingers through the space at his wrists and told him how handsome he looked. He does tonight, too.

"I'm sorry," I say.

He looks up at me and I think he's going to say something. Something mean or cruel or heartbreakingly true, but instead he says, "I just want you to know I'm aware you're paying Jessica to hang out with me."

I look up at him. I see just the slightest glint in his eye.

"What?"

"If there is one thing this whole experience has taught us, PG, it's that you are the world's worst liar."

I fumble for words. The sound of my nickname on his lips like that feels like a balm. This is the most he's spoken to me since we broke up. "I'm not," I say. "Paying her, I mean."

Rainer raises his eyebrows at me.

"Turns out some girls will hang out with you without receiving a dime."

Rainer sweeps his lips to the side. "Some girls."

Jessica comes into the room wearing a black dress, black ballet flats, and a jean jacket. Her hair is up in a ponytail and you can clearly see the blue emerald-drop earrings she has on. She looks stunning.

"You look great," I tell her. "I have to borrow those earrings sometime."

She blushes. "You sure you won't come?"

I glance at Rainer. He's putting some cash from his

back pocket into his wallet. I know sooner or later we're going to have to start hanging out. Sooner or later we're going to have to decide how to move forward.

But not tonight. Not here. Not yet.

"I'm sure," I say. "Have fun."

They leave and I get my new key. "We'll have your things packed and transferred," the bellman tells me.

I take the opposite elevators up to the fifteenth floor. The lights in Tokyo are amazing and our hotel is all glass. You can get a 360 degree view of the city.

I take off my leather pants and red top and slide into a hotel bathrobe. Heaven. I flip through the room service menu and am just about to order everything on it when the doorbell rings. My suitcases. Filled with all kinds of crazy clothes I won't even have a chance to wear.

I open the door expecting to see a towering cart of luggage, but instead it's Jordan. Dressed in jeans and a long-sleeved grey T-shirt.

My heart start hammering straight through the terrycloth. "Hi," I say.

He nods. "Can I come in?"

I stand with my back pressed against the door as he enters. I feel the air leave my body in a solid rush when he brushes past me. The door swings closed behind us. *Click.*

"Nice view," he says, still moving towards the windows. I follow him. I catch a glimpse of myself in the hall mirror and wish I hadn't taken my clothes off. But Jordan has seen me in just a bathing suit many times before.

"What's up?" I ask him.

He doesn't turn around, just keeps looking out the window. "I don't know," he says. "I had them switch your room so you could be on the other side of the hotel. And now I'm here and . . . I don't know."

It feels like someone set off sparklers inside my chest. "You switched my room?"

He turns around. His black eyes find mine. "You didn't go out," he says.

I hold his gaze. "No," I say. "I didn't."

Suddenly everything I've held in for the last few weeks starts bubbling up to the surface. Our talk in my bed and those photos and the breakup with Rainer and the tabloid story and Alexis—the truth that she hid from me. And Jordan—always, Jordan. Jordan there, buzzing in the background like white noise. Jordan filling my head. Jordan in my dreams. Jordan here, now.

But I don't have time to say any of it because in the next moment he's closing the space between us.

He takes my face gently in his hands and touches his lips to mine. But almost before they meet he's drawing me in tighter. His hands work down my back. His lips are urgent on mine—fierce, pressing, like he's trying to tell me something with their movement. I reach up and feel his neck, his jaw. I let my hands explore his face. The curve of his neck, the smooth skin below his ear, where his silver scar still sits. He pulls me in closer so we're chest to chest. I can feel his heart, wild and free, against my own.

We keep kissing as he angles me towards the bed. We crash onto it, my lips never leaving his.

I can't breathe. I swear soon I will be swallowed up in darkness, but I don't care. Jordan's mouth on mine is hot and wet and desperate. I have no idea how I could possibly have gone so long without him. How I could possibly not have suffocated without him near me. It feels insane that we've somehow been able to stay away from each other.

His fingers find my sides, sliding me up to the pillows. My hands dig into his shoulders. I feel the creases of his muscles, the knots down his back. He moans out into my mouth and I arch up against him.

His lips leave mine and find my collarbone. He pulls impatiently at the top of my robe and edges it down around my shoulders. He kisses my neck, my cheek, right below my ear. I gasp and dig my fingers into his back and then down, towards the hem of his T-shirt. They slide up underneath, like they're working on their own. I feel his skin—hot and soft. He inhales sharply as my fingers graze over his abs.

"Paige," he whispers.

My hands trail down again. For one brief moment his eyes meet mine. *Whatever you want,* they seem to say.

I pull his shirt up and then he's lifting it over his head and letting it fall to the floor.

He's above me and I sit up, placing my hands gently on his shoulders and letting them wander down. I feel his biceps move, the hard muscles under his skin flex and release. He's so beautiful. I want to tell him. I want to tell him a million things.

His hands are back on my neck. He's touching whatever skin is exposed, which isn't a lot, considering this bathrobe is like the size of Texas.

I pull at the tie at my waist and then Jordan covers my hands with his own. His eyes look into mine and I know what he's asking, but I just reach up and kiss him and as I do the bathrobe loosens and Jordan gently opens it, sliding it down off my shoulders until it pools around me on the bed.

I'm completely naked, and as soon as the robe is by my sides I have the distinct, immediate urge to cover myself. But Jordan won't let me. "Don't," he says. "Please let me see you."

He takes my hands firmly in his and puts them on his face and then he runs his own up and down my back. The feeling of his fingers on my bare skin makes me shiver against him. I press my lips to his temple and then the robe is forgotten, lost in the sheets, and we're skin to skin.

Jordan runs a hand through my hair. He edges me off

of him, just slightly. "You're so incredibly beautiful," he says. I feel his gaze on me and it makes my whole body blush. I don't know what to say, so instead I lean forward and kiss him.

It feels painfully good. Our veins are electric wires. I want to touch him everywhere, and I know he feels the same way because our hands can't move fast enough. I run them over his skin marveling at how his breath constricts and expands based on where I touch him. I love that I have this effect on him. It's heady, weightless. It makes me feel powerful in a way I never have before.

I let my fingers dip into the top of his jeans and he grips my hips tightly and groans into my shoulder.

I can't catch my breath. I fumble with the clasp on his belt. I want to remove every remaining barrier between us.

He picks his head up and our eyes meet. My hands are still at his hips. "I want . . ." I start. I feel his body tense above mine and then he's touching my cheek. He runs his thumb back and forth across the skin.

"Tell me," he says. His voice is strained. "Tell me what you want."

Everything. I want everything. I want to go somewhere with him I've never been with anyone before. I want to close my eyes and just feel him. Be with him. For one night I want us to be the only two people in the world.

But then it comes in—the dark cloud of reality. I see

it cover my face and then his until it leaves us both in shadows. We're not. We're not the only two people in the world.

Photos of us barely touching sent everything into a tailspin. And I know no one is here, now. I know it's just us. But tomorrow it won't be. Tomorrow it will be Rainer and Jessica and then L.A. and Sandy and Greg—this whole universe where we're not alone. Where we can't be.

"I want you," I say. "So much. You have to know that." I run my hand over his forehead. I don't want to say what I have to next: "But we can't."

Jordan sits up. He pulls me with him. "No," he says. He shakes his head. "Paige, I—that stuff I said before, about letting you go? I was wrong."

I close my eyes. I feel the tears come and I will them away. "You weren't," I say.

He picks my chin up and kisses me softly on the lips. My eyes flutter open. I see his—those deep, dark pools of intensity. I can't look away when he says: "I just wanted one night."

"I know," I whisper. "But if you stay here and we do this what is tomorrow going to be like?"

"I don't care about tomorrow." His black eyes look into mine and they're so beautiful, so pained, I want to weep.

I kiss his forehead. His cheek. The edge of his temple. "You do," I whisper. "This would just make it worse."

"How much worse can it get?" he says. His face flushes and for a moment I'm afraid. I see his helpless anger flair and then retreat. "The world hates me. They think I broke up the Golden Couple—and maybe I did. I've been trying to prove something to Rainer, to get his friendship back, but I'm just tired. I'm tired of lying to him and you and mostly myself. Because the truth is we haven't been friends in a really, really long time. What we had, back when we were brothers? That was lifetimes ago. We're never going to get back there. Too much has happened."

"It isn't irreversible," I protest. I know how much they once meant to each other. That kind of love doesn't go away.

Jordan takes my hands in his. "It's never going to be what you want it to be because we're both always going to want you."

I think about Rainer's words. *I don't think that makes you confused, Paige. I think that makes you selfish.*

"This is my fault," I say. "I called you. I betrayed him. You tried to stay away and I just . . . You were right when you said we needed time. We should be taking time."

"No," Jordan says. His words are fierce, determined. "*I* moved your room. *I* came here tonight. No amount of time is going to fix this because I don't want it fixed. I don't want it to go away. Paige, can't you see? I'm in love with you."

168

Love. Four letters. One syllable. It's the thing I have wanted to hear from him since that night on the beach. Possibly even since I met him. I have wanted it so badly that I didn't even dare dream about it. I haven't let myself think about what it would be like to hear it from him because it seemed like it would never happen. That it couldn't.

I'm about to answer. To say, instinctively, what I feel, too, when the doorbell rings. My eyes go wide and I scramble to put my robe back on. My first thought is: Rainer.

I don't tell him to, but Jordan hangs back. I walk to the door, take a deep breath, and open it.

But it's just the bellman. My suitcases. Those goddamn suitcases. I hold the door open as he carries and deposits them into the walk-in closet off the hallway.

I find my wallet on the minibar counter and press a bill into his hand. "Thank you," I say.

The door closes and I hear Jordan move out from the darkness behind me. I exhale and turn around. The lights from the window are casting shadows on his face, so his eyes are hidden. I want to cross the room, take his hand, and pull him into the light. I want to pick up exactly where we left off. To tell him I love him, too. Of course I do.

But this last moment is like a bucket of cold water splashed straight to the face—*wake up*—and as I turn to him I realize something. I realize the way I feel about him.

Love, yes, but something else, too. Responsibility. I want to help him, I always have. Just like Rainer has always wanted to help me.

When Jordan first got to set, I wanted to make things better. For Rainer, at first, but then for Jordan. I wanted to understand him. Then I wanted to protect him from the way I felt about Rainer. I wanted to make fame easier for him, his past less painful. I wanted to put my arms around him and make it better. But I can't. Because I can't see him in the light. I can't be *seen* with him the light. And he needs to be with someone who can.

"Jordan . . ." I start, but he just shakes his head.

"Don't," he says.

I steady my voice. I can feel my heartbeat in my ears. "Jordan, you have no idea what that means to me."

"But you don't feel the same way."

I gawk at him. "Are you serious?"

He's put his shirt back on and I feel something tighten in my stomach, thinking of how close we were just minutes ago.

"Jordan, the problem isn't not loving you. The problem is what to do with the very real fact that I do."

We're silent for a moment and I feel the distance extend out between us like the horizon. Because that isn't all I have to say. "From the moment we met I feel like we've just been torturing each other. And I don't want that for either one of us anymore. Do you see what this has created? You and Rainer . . ."

"You have to get over that," Jordan says. He sounds almost angry. His jaw is locked. "It's not your problem what my relationship is like with Rainer."

"Yes," I say. "It is. I care about you, and I know you care about each other."

"Paige," Jordan says, his tone softening slightly. "Let me and Rainer worry about me and Rainer."

"And what about me?" I say. "I'm sorry to sound selfish, Jordan, but the fact that I'm hurting both of you is not making me feel great. I feel terrible, all the time."

"These last few weeks have been rough," Jordan says. "Those tabloids are the devil. I told you they'll make anything up."

"But they didn't make this up!" I'm practically yelling now and Jordan stops and looks at me, surprised. "Sure, those pictures weren't what they looked like, but, Jordan, it *was* romantic. It *wasn't* okay. They were right."

Jordan shakes his head. "Do you know what you're saying?"

"I'm not saying it's okay that we're followed. But I'm trying to acknowledge the fact that we *are*. We don't live in a world where we can just feel what we want to feel and act how we want to act and not have there be consequences."

"I'll take the consequences," Jordan says.

"I won't."

I take a step towards him and his face comes out of the shadows. I see how tired he is. There are dark circles under his bloodshot eyes.

"No one is winning," I say softly.

Jordan stands perfectly still. "So that's it?"

I stuff my hands down into the terrycloth pockets. "Yeah," I say. "That's it."

Jordan looks at me in disbelief. But then his face changes. I see the Jordan I met on Maui—the one who was hard and closed. It breaks my heart straight in half.

"If that's what you want," he says.

I want to tell him it's not what I want. How could it possibly be what I want? What I want is to cross the room and let him take me back into his arms. What I want is to have met him first. What I want is for Rainer and Jordan not to be so important to me—to each other. But none of those things are a reality.

"I'm going to go home," Jordan says. "I can't stay here."

"We have two days left. What am I going to tell people?"

Jordan runs a hand over his forehead. "Make something up," he says. "You seem to be pretty good at excuses lately." His words are cold and I pull my robe tighter around me, feeling the chill.

He starts towards me. It's taking all the self-control I

can muster to stay stuck to the spot. If I feel him again, I know I won't be able to say no.

But he doesn't stop. He walks right past me and out the door.

I hear it click behind him. Silence. I look at the ten suitcases in the closet. The crumpled bed. And then I let myself slide down to the floor. I put my head on my knees, and for not the first time in recent memory, I cry.

CHAPTER 13

The next two days are fine. That's all I can say now: fine. Not bad, not great, not anything. Just, fine. Numb, maybe. Rainer seems in increasingly good spirits, probably due to Jordan's absence. Jessica, per request, is spending a lot of time with him. He drags her on all kinds of tours and to shows. We do two other appearances and a series of interviews.

No one seems too concerned with Jordan's absence but none of our usual handlers are here. Something tells me Tawny and Sandy wouldn't be as cool with him just bailing.

It's not until the plane ride home that Rainer and I actually talk. I'm surprised when I see him come over and take the seat next to me.

"I need to ask you something," he says, his hands on his knees. "Why did Jordan leave?"

I close my eyes. I don't feel up for lying. Not after these last few days. "I told you, he had some family thing or something. I don't really know."

Rainer sighs. "Listen, I'm trying to figure out a diplomatic, non-douchebag way of asking you what's going on with you two."

I shake my head. "Do you really want to know?"

"Yes. I'd like you to tell me the truth."

"So ask me."

"Are you together?"

I run a hand over my forehead. "No."

"Okay." The relief in his voice makes me wince.

I look up at him. His eyes are focused on me now, intently. "But, Rainer?"

"Yeah?" he says, swallowing.

"We might be if I wasn't so afraid of losing you."

Rainer takes this in. "That's so unfair," he says. But it's not bitter, just regretful.

"I know," I say, tucking my hands between my knees.

"Can we just agree," he says. "That we won't do anything, we won't date anyone else, until we figure this out?"

I look up at him. His eyes are bright, clear. I want so much to see myself there. "Yeah," I say. "We can do that."

We fly through the day. I sleep off and on. Jessica

and Rainer watch movies. We land at LAX a little before midnight. We flew commercial home so now we have to deal with the photographers outside.

Jessica goes ahead to make sure the car is there and Rainer pulls me to the side as we deplane. "What do you want to do?" he asks.

I tuck a piece of stray hair back up into my baseball hat. I see our fellow passengers glancing at us as they pass by. "What do you mean?"

Rainer inhales. "Do you want to walk out together?"

I look up at him. His face is open, relaxed. No hat or sunglasses. He's offering himself to me as protection. Do I want to take it?

"It'll make things easier if you take my hand," he says.

He holds it out to me. I'm exhausted, and all I want to do is just slip my palm into his. To let him lead me down, through the photographers. It would put a rest to this disastrous public image if we just do this one, simple thing. Back together. What cheating scandal? It's all behind us. We're solid. Throw all the rocks you want.

But I can't. I'm not even sure why he's offering it. Is it because he wants to protect me, or because he wants to cement us further together in the public eye? Either way, I have to say no.

I shake my head. "We have to do it on our own," I say.

Rainer nods once. Curt. And then he steps ahead of me.

Sure enough, they are gathered when we descend the escalator. They scream obscene things at us.

"Rainer! Have you ditched your cheater girlfriend yet?"

"Paige! Where is your lover, Jordan?"

But I keep my head up. I don't answer. I just keep thinking about three minutes. It's only ever three minutes. And sure enough, it turns out to be true.

I used to think that speaking up, speaking your mind, was the most powerful thing you could do—saying what you think and feel. But I'm beginning to learn there is a real power in what you don't say. There is power in holding yourself above the need to clarify, or apologize. Just being who you are, no explanation necessary.

Photographers aren't the only ones who have greeted us on the ground. Fans are there, too. They hold up banners and headshots. "Can we take a picture?" three girls a few years younger ask.

"Sure," I say.

We pose together and someone else surrounding us takes the iPhone pic. And then I do one with her and one of the girls reciprocates. "We love you," the girls say. "We support you, no matter what." They're strangers, I know. They don't know me or Rainer or Jordan, but as I thank them I can't help feeling good inside. I can't help but feel like they mean it. Maybe not everyone feeds off our drama. Maybe some people really want us to be happy.

Sandy greets me in my town car. The cameras are still flashing, but I can see her smiling at me. "Hey, PG," she says. "Guess what?"

I keep my head down. "Do I want to know?"

We start driving away and I collapse against the back seat. "Oh yeah," she says. "You do." I look at her. She's wearing a quirky smile on her face, her lips pursed together. "Tomorrow you're going for the *Closer to Heaven* audition. Fox got involved and I think that coupled with your recent display of together-ness with the guys . . ." She smiles wide. "They've changed their tune about you."

I sit up immediately. "Really?"

"Really. Amanda came through. It's not a sure thing, but I think you have a real shot."

"This is amazing."

"Amazing and not everything. We still need to sit down and look seriously at the scripts Amanda has been sending."

I close my eyes, already thinking about how I'm going to nail this thing tomorrow. "Okay," I say. "Whatever you want. Put me in a cat suit. I don't care."

"You do care," Sandy says. "And that is what's going to make you a great actress. But we all have to make sacrifices."

I peel one eye open at her. "I'm getting that," I say.

Sandy pats my shoulder. "You're doing okay, kid," she says.

*

I wake up at the crack of dawn the next morning. I went back to the Beverly Hills apartment. I hadn't stayed here or even set foot here since we got back to L.A. post tour, but Sandy had it cleaned and outfitted with groceries for me. "I figured you may want the option," she told me in the car. I know Rainer moved back into the Bel Air house while I was in Malibu, so she was right.

It was weird to stay here alone. When we got back from press tour, I was so scared to be by myself. I wanted to be by Rainer's side at all times. The thought of being at this apartment, alone, made me feel like I might as well have been standing on the walk of fame inviting in every stranger in sight. But coming home to the quiet, sleeping in the bed by myself, doesn't feel like punishment. It feels good. It feels like here, alone, is exactly where I need to be.

I sift through the mail that has built up in my absence. Some bills, magazines I immediately deposit into the trash, a rehearsal dinner invitation for Joanna's swiftly approaching wedding. It has pink and red swirls on it and I can't help but laugh. Her poor future husband has no say already.

I take my coffee cup outside and settle into a chair on the patio. It's chilly now, with the sun not fully up, and I pop the hood on my sweatshirt over my head. I tuck my knees up onto my chest, letting the steam from the coffee fog up my face.

My phone rings. I take it out of my pocket and smile when I see Alexis's name flashing on the screen. "It's six thirty," I say when I pick up.

"And I've already meditated, done yoga, and made a green juice. What do you have to show for your morning?"

I laugh. "What's up?"

"I missed you last night. Where are you?"

"The Beverly Hills apartment," I say.

"Oh how the mighty have fallen," Alexis says. "But I feel you. Georgina and Blake are coming to claim Malibu for a few weeks so I'm moving back home, too." She gets quiet on the other end for a moment. "And Jordan and I broke up," she says.

"Broke up?"

"*Publicly*, obviously. I issued a statement that we split amicably. They'll probably think it has something to do with you, but it's been enough time that it shouldn't be too terrible."

"Wow," I say. I take a breath and ask what I want to know. "Alexis . . . *is* there someone you want to date?"

I hear Alexis clear her throat. "I just want to start limiting the lies, you know?"

"Yes, I know." I think of Rainer and I on the plane. It may suck now, but in some ways it's better. At least we're finally being honest. "I'm proud of you," I say. It seems a silly thing to say, but it's true. I all at once feel an overwhelming affection for Alexis.

She laughs. "You're so terribly American," she says. "All feelings. Anyway I have to run. I have a meeting with the Do Something people. Did I tell you I'm doing their new anti-bullying campaign?"

Do Something is one of the largest organizations for young people. They cover every social cause, and I know Alexis has been gunning hard to have a bigger role with them.

"That's amazing!" I say. "Congrats. They're lucky to have you." I make a mental note to email Jake about this. Maybe she can help him cast a wider net with his environmental outreach.

"I'm lining up a ton of school visits and events and even some counseling sessions. I'm excited about it."

"That's so great, Alexis."

"Thanks. Anyway head out to the beach if you want to. It's supposed to be a gorgeous day. Might as well capitalize on it while we can."

"I can't," I say, smiling to myself. "I have an audition."

"Ah! Keep me posted, gorgeous!" she says, and hangs up.

I finish my coffee, and get dressed. I put on a white lace top and jeans. I blow dry my hair and apply a little mascara and a thin layer of lip-gloss from one of the makeup kits that is in my suitcases.

At eight thirty I get in the rental car and drive out. There are a few paparazzi there, and they get some photos, but it doesn't really bother me. I'm too excited about today to care.

I call Sandy from the car.

"Ask for James Santiago. They're expecting you, of course. And make sure you go in the Galaxy Gate. The lot can be confusing."

"Thanks."

"I hope you kill it!" Sandy says.

"I don't totally believe you."

"Hey," Sandy says. "I want what you want."

Studio lots are confusing, to put it mildly. I find The Galaxy Gate, but it involves making, like, two and a half illegal U-turns and by the time I actually locate a parking spot I feel like I've been circling half my life.

They gave me some VIP access pass, but I couldn't find any of the VIP spots so I end up in a parking-garage the size of my old high school.

I write the floor level of my spot on the inside of my wrist with a sharpie from the center console and take the elevator down to the ground floor. I end up outside, in a grassy area with some scattered tables. There is a café off to the side and people come in and out ferrying coffees.

A few of them glance up but then go back to meeting or talking on their cell phones. That's the nice thing about Hollywood—once you're inside the gates, no one cares that you're famous.

I ask a passing girl carrying a stack of scripts for directions to suite 400, and she offers to walk me over. Her name is Ireeka. She's wearing a name tag, but she introduces herself anyway. She's short, with brown hair that is knotted at the base of her neck. "I'm surprised you're here alone," she says as we walk.

I shrug. "People think you become famous and are then incapable of walking."

Ireeka raises an eyebrow at me. "Don't you?"

It makes me laugh, which is good, because the closer we get to suite 400 the more nervous I am becoming.

"What are you here for?" Ireeka asks me. She directs me with her arm to make a left.

"Audition."

"You still have to do that?"

"Sometimes," I say. "When they don't think you're right for a part."

Ireeka rolls her eyes. She stops in front of an office building that looks kinda like a trailer—long and flat. "Suite 400," she says. "You've arrived."

"Thank you for helping me out."

I turn to start climbing the stairs when Ireeka stops me.

"I think you're good," she says. "I mean *Locked* wasn't my thing, but you weren't bad."

I laugh. "Thanks?"

She shrugs. "You're an actress," she says. "Show them you know how to be someone else."

She gives me a small wave and flags down someone passing by in a golf cart. "Tony, give me a lift."

I turn away from her and pop the door open.

I'm greeted by two young assistants sitting in front of parallel offices, both with their doors open. A ball flies out of the office, one of the assistants catches it, and tosses it back inside.

On the walls are posters of movies I love. *Now and Then* and my favorite from a few years ago: *The Spectacular Now*.

"Paige," the assistant who isn't tossing the ball says. "You're here."

She stands up to come around the front of her desk. She's dressed in a short mini skirt, leggings, and cowboy boots. "Kiernan, knock it off."

"Paige is here!" Kiernan yells. He gives me a lopsided smile. "Can we get you anything? Water? Coffee? Vodka?"

I look from the girl to him. "He's joking," she says. "We only have tequila on weekdays. We're professionals."

"Barely." The guy who I know is James strides out of his office. He's younger than I expected—maybe 30ish.

He's wearing jeans and a *Back to the Future* T-shirt. "Paige Townsen," he says. "We're delighted you're here."

He holds out his hand to me. It's warm and welcoming. "Everyone is gathered in my office. Come on back."

"Thanks," I say.

I follow James past Kiernan and into his office. It's small, same vibe as outside. On his couch are three people—a woman and two men. One of them has his feet up on the coffee table. All of them are dressed casually, sipping on Starbucks to-go cups. They look up when we enter.

"Everyone, this is Paige Townsen," James says. "Paige, this is Billy Zack, our director. Carl Cohen, my producing partner, and that's Irina Tell, the woman responsible for writing this thing we're told you love so much."

"It's a brilliant script," I say.

Irina smiles. "I'm glad you think so. Have a seat."

James pulls his swivel chair out from his desk and gestures for me to sit down. Everything is so casual, so no big deal, it almost makes me forget why I'm here.

Billy speaks first. He's a tall guy, wiry, with black hair and small blue eyes. "I know you had to fight the good fight to get here," Billy says. "And we all appreciate that."

Carl and James nod.

"The thing with this character is that she's a pretty broken girl. We're talking child abuse, abandonment. It's heavy shit. I'm not saying you can't handle it, but it would be a break from tradition, let's say."

"I'm up for the challenge," I say. "I want to do projects I'm passionate about—that's why I got into this business."

Carl and James exchange a look. Irina writes something down. "Please," I continue. "I know that sounds like a stock answer, but it's not. I think you're probably aware my reps don't even want me here."

Billy laughs. "That's a ringing endorsement, frankly."

"I fell in love with this script. It's like nothing I have read before. There are piles of—" I look at the group— "*stuff*, on my agent's desk and none of it is even a fourth as good as this."

Billy looks at Irina. "It *is* a pretty kick-ass script."

"Why thank you."

"And I know if you gave me a shot I would be perfect for this. Maybe you can't see it but I can. I promise. I'm your girl."

Why don't you read for us?" Irina asks. I can't tell if she's impressed or embarrassed by my outpouring of emotion.

James nods. "That's why we're here."

He hands me a script, but I shake my head. "I memorized the whole thing," I say. "Just give me a scene."

James looks impressed. "Billy?"

"Let's jump right into the belly," he says. "Why don't you give us the first live audience scene?"

I suppress a smile. I was hoping they would choose this one. It's one of the scenes I know the best.

I stand up and roll out my neck. And then I begin.

The last audition I did was for *Locked*. I remember stepping into that room—one so much bigger than this. With casting directors and producers and Rainer. I think about how much I relied on him in that audition. It wasn't even me acting. It was *us*. It was the chemistry we have. The way we can just kind of fold into each other in a scene. I know I got the part because he was there, but I don't think I've realized until this moment, reading these lines for Billy and Carl and James and Irina, how much that's held me back. If I got the role because of Rainer, it means I wouldn't have gotten it on my own—that maybe I'm not a good enough actress by myself. And it's this lingering fear—a fear I need to prove *wrong*—that drives the scene. I know now why this role is so important. I can't just be handed something else. I need to earn it. I need to earn *this*.

"That was great," Irina says when I finish. "You're a talent."

I exhale all the breath I've been holding.

Billy nods. "I mean you're going to have to meet with Susan."

"Studio head," James says, before I can ask.

"But you're a find," Carl says. He swings his feet off the coffee table. "We're not going to lie to you—there are three other actresses in the running right now that the studio is very interested in. You've got some competition."

I nod. "I assumed," I say. I don't think I'm doing a very good job of hiding my disappointment.

"But we're fans," James says. "You don't have to worry about that."

Billy stands up and takes my hand. His grip is strong as he shakes it. "We'll see you back with Susan," he says.

Irina and Carl extend their hands, too. "Great work."

James walks me out, back to the assistants who are now playing catch with each other. "Is someone making a coffee run?" he asks them.

Kiernan looks up. "On it." He stands and pops a credit card into his back pocket. "See ya," he says to me, and charges out the door.

"He's untrained," the girl says. "Sorry."

James laughs. "Do you need someone to walk you out?"

I shake my head. "I can figure it out." I followed Ireeka pretty closely. I can easily get back. But that's not why I say no. I kind of want to explore, just a little bit, on my own.

James holds the door open for me. "I have a good feeling," he says.

"Does that come in writing?"

He laughs. "Not quite, unfortunately." He pats me on the shoulder. "We'll talk soon."

The parking garage is around to the right, but instead

when I get outside I make a left. I follow the pathway up past trailers and people milling around. Some of them look at me, two even come over and offer me assistance, but I just shake my head and tell them I know where I'm going.

I end up in New York. There is a part of the lot that is a makeshift Manhattan. The west village, I think, but I only know that from old *Friends* re-runs. We went to New York on the press tour, but I mostly just saw the inside of the Soho Grand and the sets of talk shows.

This New York is all brownstones and cute walk-up buildings. Old-school traffic lights that hang overhead.

I take a seat on a stoop and exhale out. The whole of New York is just a block long and right now, no one is here. I wanted to go out when we were in New York, but there wasn't any time, and Tawny said it would be too crazy. And all I wanted was a moment like this one to soak in the city.

I know this isn't New York, not even close, but it's like that old saying—you get what you need?

I sit with my hands on my knees for another twenty minutes, until my butt starts to feel sore. And then I find my way back to the parking garage, check my wrist, and take the elevator up to the third level.

I dial Sandy from the car and fill her in.

"So what now?" she says when I finish.

"Call Amanda," I say. "I'm ready to work."

CHAPTER 14

My sister's wedding is a month later. It seems to come out of nowhere and when my mom reminds me that I need to book my ticket home I immediately feel guilty. My sister and I have been talking more these last few months, but I'm Joanna's maid of honor and besides some phone calls I haven't been much help. Not with the planning. Not with the bachelorette. Not to look after Annabelle the way I would have done while Joanna and my mom ran wedding errands. I didn't even order my own dress. Jessica did that for me, as a favor. Along with a Just Like Me doll to give to Annabelle for her birthday. I need some face-time with my family, before my niece forgets I exist.

I mean, in my pitiful defense, this month has been crazy. Prep for the second *Locked* and meetings with nearly every studio exec in the business. We've lined up three new projects in as many weeks. Things both Amanda and I agree on, even if I have been appeasing her a little. My head is spinning, but it's good motion. Staying busy is the key, I've realized, to moving forward.

Tonight I'm headed to Portland without Rainer. He was going to be my date, back when he was, well, my boyfriend. Alexis is going with Georgina to New York for upfronts. I'm glad we're all leaving at the same time. They're the only people I hang out with anymore. I've seen Rainer just a few times. He moved back into the Bel Air house. He's going out. We may be unfinished, but we don't seem doomed. We're keeping our promise. I don't see him out with other girls and I'm not in touch with Jordan. I've even resisted the urge to Google stalk him online. No good can come of that.

"What's the deal with your sister?" Georgina asks. We're at lunch. This vegan place called Café Gratitude in West Hollywood. Jake would love it here. I, however, suffer through tempeh in silence.

Tailor is with us. I've properly met her since the night of the MTV Movie Awards—turns out she's the star of *Locked*'s competing franchise about demons. She's friends with Georgina, but Alexis thinks she's intolerable. Personally, I think she's kind of boring. She always needs to be so pretty and perfect. Her stylist chooses what she wears to the gym.

"She's not bad," I say. The truth is I'm not entirely sure how to answer that question. My sister used to be selfish and absent, but she's changed since Annabelle, and over the course of this last year. It's like me being gone made us closer. It's not like we're best friends, or anything, but I've even started to miss Joanna a little bit, although it could be magnified guilt over not being there to help out at home.

"I wish you were coming to New York," Alexis says. "I'm going to be so bored while this one—" she elbows Georgina—"does press events all day."

"I went to upfronts one year!" Tailor squeals. "The CW party rocked."

"You only think that because you hooked up with Dave Marsh that night," Georgina says, making a face like she's just smelled fish.

Alexis rolls her eyes, and it's not that inconspicuous.

"My second to last upfronts," Georgina says. She leans down and takes a long drag of her spirulina juice. Gross. She looks at me from underneath her lashes. "Then I will be out here all the time with you guys."

I don't mention the fact that we're leaving—soon. We start shooting three weeks after the wedding. Three weeks, and we'll be back on Maui. All of us. Me. Jordan. Rainer and Alexis—who continues to remain a neutral third party. She and Jordan may have "broken up" but they're still friends. I don't ask her about him, though. I don't want to put her in an awkward position.

"What's the latest on *Closer*?" Alexis asks.

I knee her under the table. Word has leaked that I'm up for the role, but I still haven't met with Susan. They keep postponing. I have a string of emails from James telling me to "keep the faith." I haven't heard a peep on it since.

"I don't know," I say. "I'm hoping I still have a shot."

"I heard you're jumping through hoops for that project," Tailor says. "Why?"

I spear a piece of kale. "I love it."

"You guys are so lucky," Georgina says wistfully. "If I didn't have to shoot a million weekends a year . . ."

"Oh come on," Alexis says. "You adore it. Stop whining."

"It's true," Tailor pipes up. "That's why I never tried TV."

"You never tried TV because the first thing you ever did was a movie with George Clooney," Georgina says.

Tailor nods, like *fair*.

There are photographers around. They're snapping our photos from the street. I've gotten used to chewing with my mouth closed. I try and always smile, but I know I fail at that, too. There are still articles daily about how I'm "coping" with the loss of Rainer. One photographer caught me sneezing last week and it looked kind of like I was crying, which was good enough for them.

Paige Mourns Raige

Georgina lowers her voice and motions for us to all lean in. "It's not working with Blake," she says.

Alexis eyes her. "What are you saying?"

Georgina bites her lip. Her auburn hair falls just slightly in her face. I have the distinct impression that even this, this confession, is staged. It's like she's doing a scene from her show.

"But you two are so cute!" Tailor chirps. She's currently dating the lead singer from that English boy band. The one with five guys I can't tell apart. Their music is catchy, though.

"He's too old for me," she says.

"He's not that much older than Rainer," Alexis points out.

"And that turned out so well." Georgina looks at me. "No offense."

"None taken."

"It's just complicated," she says. "We want different things. For instance he wants to be there and I want to be here."

"Aren't Cassy and Damien about to get together on the show?" I ask.

I'm almost through *Elsewhere* and hooked. It's super sexy. They get hot and heavy weekly. I can only imagine what her consummation scene with Blake will entail.

"Yeah," she says, setting her fork down.

"That sucks," I say. "But if you break up, how are you going to film all that stuff? Won't that be awkward?"

The three of them look at me. Alexis's face is incredulous.

"What?"

"I don't know," she says, sitting back. "How are *you* going to do it?"

I look around the table. All three of them are looking at me with raised eyebrows.

"Darling," Alexis says. "You've read the second *Locked*, right?"

"Yes." But then it dawns on me, what they're talking about. I've been so busy trying to figure out the fallout of my relationship with Rainer that I didn't stop to consider what actually happens in book two.

Book two is all August and Ed. It's me and Jordan. It's him trying to win her back.

"Crap."

Alexis sits back and smiles. "Good luck with that."

Georgina glances at Tailor. "Don't ever fall for James," she says, referencing her co-star.

"Can't," Tailor says, downing a wheatgrass shot. "He's gay."

"But isn't he hooking up with Lindsay?" I ask.

Alexis picks at her plate. "It's not real," she whispers.

Georgina slings her arm over Alexis's shoulder. "We're messes," she says.

"Hot messes," Alexis corrects, leaning her head on Georgina's. The gesture makes me immediately miss Cassandra. It's a pain I feel often, and always seemingly out of nowhere. But how could it be out of nowhere? She's still right here, even if I've been keeping her at an arm's length. That's the thing about the people you love—they don't really go away.

"Anyone want to go to Bungalow tonight?" Tailor asks. "It's Alessandra's birthday. I think she closed it."

Alexis picks her head up and yawns. "Can't. I have training." She looks at me. "I still can't believe we start shooting so soon."

"I'm so happy you're going to be there for longer than a few days this time," I say.

"Beach days!"

"Not quite," I say. "But you remember, just shooting there is pretty awesome."

I'm not there this time as long as I'd like to be. Only for a month, then Jordan and I fly to Seattle to shoot the rest of the second film. Rainer and Alexis will be in and out.

"Let's pay," Georgina says. "I have to pack."

"Me too," I say. I'm trying to remember where my shoes and bridesmaid dress are.

"I already took care of it," Tailor says. She waves at the

waiter, who gives her a little nod.

We make our way down the steps and wait for the valet to bring Tailor's car around.

I tuck my chin to my chest and cross my arms. The paparazzi are yelling at all of us, but I see them angle towards me. That's a strange thing. That in this group, I'm the most famous. The photo of me will go for more than the one of Tailor or Georgina or Alexis.

Some of it is the scandal, but most of it is *Locked*. It's bigger than anything else. I don't know whether I feel pride or shame at that. Both, probably.

Tailor's car comes around and Georgina gets in front, Alexis and I behind.

"That was intense," Tailor says as she makes a left onto Melrose.

"You think?" I say. "That's nothing compared to what it was a few weeks ago."

Alexis squeezes my shoulder. "They've been cruel," she says.

Tailor flashes me a sympathetic smile in the rearview.

"What time is your flight?" Georgina asks me.

"Nine," I say. "I have to help my mom with the rehearsal dinner tomorrow. We're hosting."

"Isn't that traditionally the groom's responsibility?" Tailor asks.

"I guess. But the groom's family hasn't really spoken to

either of them since my sister got pregnant."

"Families are so fucked up," Georgina offers.

I think about the legal battle Rainer is currently in the middle of with his father, the details of which I'm not even sure of anymore. Lately, I've been feeling pretty lucky to have the family that I do. Sure my sister and I are different, and my brothers still treat me like a football, but at least we're not actively trying to screw each other over.

"Do you mind dropping me off in Beverly Hills?" I ask.

Tailor nods. "No problem. Do you have a ride to the airport?"

I hadn't even thought about it. "I'll call a cab."

"I'll send over a driver," Alexis says, nodding at me. "Nicer and more discreet."

When they stop in front of the house, Alexis gets out and pulls me into a hug. "Have fun," she says.

"I will." And I think it might be true. I'm excited to be back in Portland, and even to see my sister. For the first time in a long time, I'm ready to go home.

Whether home is ready for me, or even aware of me, is another story entirely. No one in my house would notice me if an anvil fell on my head. I swear. It's like I'm invisible. Which given the overexposure of the last few months is totally fine by me. My sister and mom buzz around like they're on every ounce of speed on the planet.

Saturday morning there are two caterers, three servers, two handymen, six bridesmaids, my mother and two of her friends all stuffed into our house. And everyone is in motion.

The wedding is going to be in the backyard and people are setting up chairs and erecting an arch where our swing-set used to be—it's made up entirely of daisies, my sister's favorite.

Joanna sits in her room directing as one of her bridesmaids does her hair. My sister's hair is more blonde than red—but it still falls somewhere in between. Another friend is applying eye makeup. And they're talking animatedly about the honeymoon. Joanna and Bill are going to Vancouver for four days without Annabelle—a first.

Annabelle is downstairs with my mom and I hear her chirping. She's talking so much now it's crazy. Whole, complete sentences. There is a lot I've missed, being in L.A. Annabelle growing up is definitely one of the crappiest parts of not living in Portland anymore.

"I can't believe you're getting married!" Joanna's friend, Aliyah, squeals.

I look at my sister. Her cheeks are rosy and she's smiling ear to ear. She looks radiant—more beautiful than I have ever seen her before. I feel close to her, all of a sudden. It makes me remember a time before. Back when we were not just sisters but best friends. When she used to let me borrow her dolls and dress me up like I was one. She'd let me sleep in her bed, and tell me stories at night. Stories about princesses in faraway lands and evil queens and beautiful, fierce dragons. I think about her barking orders at Cassandra and me when we'd play tea party, just the three of us.

I feel bad about the last conversation I had with Cassandra, and the creeping doubt I feel about that tabloid piece. It's been enough that I haven't returned half a dozen of her calls. She'll be at the wedding. I still have no idea what I'm going to say to her, or even how much I can.

Aliyah stands to admire her work. "You're so hot," she tells my sister.

Joanna grabs a hand-mirror and smiles. "Good," she says. She looks over at her dress. It's hanging on the back of her bedroom door. An ivory lace affair that just sweeps the floor. "Will you help me get in it?" she asks.

At first I don't say anything, assuming she's talking to Aliyah, but then I see her looking at me.

"Me?"

She rolls her eyes. "Yes, you."

"What about mom?" I ask.

Joanna huffs out. "We have pictures in five minutes. Can you just do this one thing for your sister on her wedding day?" But she's smiling at me, and I smile back.

"I'd be honored," I say.

Aliyah and the rest of the girls file out of the room. It's just my sister and I, and I try to remember the last time we were alone together, without Annabelle or our parents or brothers. It has been too long.

I take the dress off the door and carefully unzip it. I hold it open and Joanna steps in, placing one hand on my shoulder for support. She places her arms through the sheer sleeves and then I zip it up, locking the tiny satin buttons that run from the neck down to her low back. She stands in front of the mirror and I stand behind her.

"Wow," I say.

The overall picture is stunning. Her hair is pulled up into a French twist and small wisps fall around her face. Her makeup is soft—all browns and rose tones. And she's wearing a string of pearls around her neck.

Joanna turns away from the mirror and then she does something surprising: she takes my hands in hers.

"This is the most important day of my life," she says. "And I'm so glad you're here."

"I'm really happy I'm here, too." I say.

She squeezes my hands and then drops them, turning back to the mirror. She grabs a lip-gloss off the tray of makeup and starts dabbing at her lips. "And I'm really glad you let all that stupid press stuff go. Mom said you're doing much better."

I'm trying to smooth out the blush on my cheeks in the snippet of mirror I can see. Aliyah did my make up, too, and she got a little heavy-handed with the Summer Sunset.

"It's just a part of life now," I say. "It's not easy, but I'm trying not to let it dictate every one of my moods. Otherwise, I'd end up in an insane asylum." I smile at her, relishing this moment of sisterhood, of together-ness.

Joanna purses her lips in the mirror. "I'm glad you feel that way because I've been wanting to come clean. You know the story was already leaked when I told them that stuff about Jake."

I drop my hand from my cheek. "What?"

Joanna doesn't turn around, but I can see her eyes shift in the mirror.

"Joanna," I say. "What exactly are you telling me?"

Joanna huffs, and pivots, bustling up her dress. "Don't get snooty with me," she says. "Sorry we don't all have millions at our disposal. Ten thousand dollars paid for your niece and I to move out of the house, you know."

"You took money from them? From the tabloids?" My voice feels small in my ears. All I can hear is the blood pounding. "It was you. You sold me out."

"Don't be so dramatic," Joanna snaps, turning back to the mirror. She pops off the lipstick top. I have the intense desire to grab it out of her hand and smear it all over her white dress. "They already had those photos.

I didn't see what the big deal was."

"Of course you didn't," I say. "You never do. You still have no idea that your actions have consequences."

"Don't talk to me about consequences," Joanna says, dabbing her lips. "You don't know the first thing about responsibility." She turns to me. I want to slap her, or scream, but my hands and face feel frozen.

"You're wrong," I say.

"Whatever," Joanna says. "I have to go get married."

And with that she yanks open the door and disappears into the hallway.

I was so stupid. My sister was there, after the premiere, in the other room. She overheard everything I said to Cassandra. And she knew about Jake. I can't believe I ever thought she had changed. I can't believe I stopped to think that for one moment she might have considered that the universe does not spin solely around her.

And then, all at once, I feel a rush of guilt so strong it eclipses even the anger. How could I have doubted Cassandra? I let myself wonder if my best friend sold me out.

I make my way downstairs. My sister is being sequestered in our parents' room. Guests are starting to arrive.

I look outside. I'm greeted by relatives and friends of my parents. They all want to congratulate and kiss me. I feel dazed. Worse than I do with flashbulbs on a red carpet. Where is Cassandra?

Funny how just a few minutes ago I was scared of seeing her. What I would say. How I would deal with feeling so guarded around her, not sure if she ratted me out. But now I just want to talk to her, hug her, make it right.

"Yo, Patrick!"

I turn around to see the two of them—Jake and Cassandra. He's wearing a suit and she has on her yellow dress with white polka dots. They look so warm and familiar I immediately feel my throat constrict.

And then I throw my arms around both their necks. "Whoa," Cassandra coughs out into my ear. "Careful with the grip. What kind of protein powder are they feeding you out there?"

I pull back and take them in, smiling widely.

"Dude," Jake says. "I can't believe your sister is getting married."

"Annabelle is almost three," Cassandra says. "Believe."

I walk with them up the aisle to seats on the right-hand side in a middle row.

Jake goes in first but Cassandra keeps standing.

"Hey . . ." she says, cautiously.

"Hi. Listen, I'm sorry about the last few weeks. Things have just been . . ."

"It's okay. You don't have to explain."

"No, I do," I say. "I want to."

"Okay, but me first."

I laugh. Cassandra's patience hasn't improved over the years. "Shoot."

"My parents are taking me to Cabo—finally!—and Jake was supposed to come, but he wants to do a habitat trip that week. I know your schedule is crazy and you might have to leave—"

"I'm in."

Cassandra stops, mouth open. "Really?"

"Yeah," I say. "I seriously cannot think of anything I'd rather do than lie on the beach with you for a week."

"Four days," she says, but she's already moving to hug me and then she starts squealing in my ear. "We have so much to catch up on."

"You have no idea," I say, holding tight.

"Paige!" I turn around to see my mom calling me from inside, motioning with her hand.

"Showtime," I say.

Cassandra plants a kiss on my cheek. "You look terrible, by the way," she says.

I look down at my dress. Blue taffeta that turns metallic when I move. "I think that's how Joanna wants it."

Cassandra rolls her eyes and sits down next to Jake, and I head back towards my mom. I want to tell her. About Joanna and that magazine and the cash. But then I look at her. She looks happy. Really happy. Happier than I have seen her in a long time.

My dad stands in front of Joanna. He whispers something into her ear and then he takes her veil and places it over her face.

My brothers jostle each other behind and Aliyah, unsurprisingly, tries to flirt with them both.

I make a move to try to get upstairs and nab my phone—but I feel my mom's hand firmly on my arm as I take the first stair.

"Where do you think you're going?"

I spin around. "Um, hairbrush?" I try.

She looks at my head. "Down here," she says. "We're doing pictures now."

We all file out front. Bill is standing in the driveway with his back to us, and Joanna goes up and taps him on the shoulder. The photographer is right there, snapping the moment as Bill turns around and sweeps Joanna up into a big hug.

"First look," my mother tells me proudly.

"What?"

"That's what it's called when he doesn't see her coming down the aisle for the first time. Better for pictures."

Bill releases Joanna and then we all stand on the lawn, bright smiles. My mom and Joanna direct as the photographer keeps snapping.

My sister sold me out. My *sister*. And she acted so casually about it. *I needed the money ... what's the problem?*

The problem is that you should be able to trust your family. The problem is that when you splay your life out in front of the world you don't think your sister is going to be the first one to lunge for the carcass.

I've offered her money. I used to do it constantly, but not anymore, because she wouldn't take it. She scoffed at me: "what am I, a charity case?" Those were her words.

The music starts and my father takes my sister's hand. "Come on, sweetheart," he says. "It's time."

We get in our processional line. Bill's brother is walking me down the aisle. A pimply kid who looks about twelve. He starts coughing uncontrollably when I slip my arm through his.

We stand up there, all of us. My mom and dad and brothers as Joanna and Bill exchange vows. Joanna promises to make Bill peanut butter and jelly every day an hour before dinner, in case she screws their meal up. Bill promises to never complain about her collection of mini soaps and to always wake up early to start the car on mornings it's cold out. They promise to love and honor each other forever. That's what they say: *forever*.

My sister is only a few years older than I am but she already has this permanent life. A child and a home and now a husband. I don't know why, or how, but Bill agrees to spend the rest of his life with her. Until death do them part. Everyone cheers.

They walk back down the aisle to "Here Comes the Sun," and then we all go inside the house for cocktails while they turn the backyard into the wedding reception area.

I grab a glass of champagne as I search for Cassandra and Jake. Joanna and Bill are in the center of the room, my mother close by them, air kissing in every different direction. They are elated—even Annabelle is smiling from where she sits perched on my mother's hip.

Then I see my father in the kitchen. I push past people and go over to him. He's fixing himself a drink—scotch, two ice cubes—same as always.

"Hey, father of the bride," I tell him.

He turns and smiles at me. He has tears in his eyes. I've never seen my dad cry, not ever. He's reserved. When he wants to express love it's always "we." "We love you." Never I.

"Dad?"

"Allergies," he tells me.

"Liar."

I put my hand on his shoulder and then I let him wrap his arms around me. I feel him kiss the top of my head. "I'm so proud of you," he says.

I pull back and look at him. "You should be telling Joanna that."

He laughs. "She's got enough of an ego," he says.

"She sold me out," I say. The words slip out. "To the tabloids. I thought it was Cassandra but it was Joanna."

My father nods. "Don't tell your mother," he says.

"Dad, did you—"

"Yes," he says. He guides me farther into the kitchen. "But you're not going to upset her."

"Upset *her*?"

"Your sister is who she is. Sometimes I don't know where she came from, but I love her. I love her just as much as I love you. Things haven't been easy for her and lord knows she's made some bad decisions, but she knows what she did was wrong. It won't happen again."

"How do you know?"

"Because I told her if it did I'd give her something to squeal about." I look at my dad. He has a twinkle in his eye. "I pay more attention than you think," he says.

"It's not fair," I tell him.

He pinches my cheek, the way I remember him doing when I was little. "Fair is overrated," he tells me. And then he picks up his scotch. "Do your old man a favor, will you?" he asks. "I'm going to duck back there." He gestures with his elbow in the direction of the bedroom. "Cover for me?"

"Dad . . ."

"I believe you owe me," he says. "I just have to check a few scores."

I laugh. "Fine."

We both look out into the crowd at Joanna. "She's happy," he says. When he says it, he seems happy, too.

I find Cassandra and Jake sitting on the stairs. Her legs are over his lap and she's talking animatedly about something. Some champagne spills out of her glass and down onto the carpeting when she gestures.

"Hey," I say. I come and sit down next to them, tucking my dress up behind me.

"Cool party," Jake says.

"My sister leaked a story about me to the tabloids," I say. "She said they gave her ten grand." I set the glass down.

"Jesus," Jake says.

Cassandra looks thoughtful. "I saw that piece about you and Jordan and this one—" She gestures to Jake. "I figured."

I look at her. I bite my lip. "She overheard us talking."

Cassandra nods. "Yeah."

There is something about the look in her eyes, steady, strong, that let's me know she knows. She knows I thought, maybe, it was her. But we don't need to talk about it. Just like I don't need to tell anyone else about my sister. What's done is done.

"She's always been pretty selfish," Jake says. "But this takes the cake."

"Ugh, cake," Cassandra says. "Do you think *we* could

be selfish and get some early slices?"

"And not spend the next two hours sitting in my backyard toasting the happy couple?"

Cassandra's eyes sparkle. "Right," she says.

"I think that could be arranged."

We sneak into the family room where I know the cake is being stored. It's a huge white monstrosity with flowers everywhere and I cut off a big square at the bottom, sticking the roses back around to try and make up for the hole. It doesn't totally work, they'll probably notice, but I can't quite feel too sorry.

Then I grab three plastic forks and lead the procession back up to my room. We settle on the floor, attacking the cake. Jake confesses it tastes like cotton candy.

"Synthetic goodness," Cassandra says.

I flick some frosting at her. She wipes it off her nose and licks her finger.

"Disgusting," Jake says.

"I can't believe you're even consuming this much processed sugar," I say through a bite.

"That's it, guilt trip him," Cassandra says, bobbing her head. "More for us."

Jake takes Cassandra's face in his hands and plants a giant sugared kiss on her. It makes me laugh. It's weird how not weird it is. If they broke up, that would be weird.

Cassandra slaps Jake away. "What should we do?" she asks.

I set my fork down. "Chutes and Ladders?"

When the three of us were younger we used to spend hours playing board games. Monopoly, Candy Land. Chutes and Ladders was Cassandra's favorite, though.

Her eyes light up. "Yes!" she says. She goes into my closet, the one she knows so well, stands on her tiptoes and reaches for the box that sits on the top shelf. She pulls it down. The lid is dust covered but inside, untouched, are all our old supplies. *The Three Musketeers Rule Book*, aka *Bob* written in Cassandra's loopy cursive. Letters to each other. An old baseball hat with our initials marked in the inside. Photographs, Valentines, and our board games.

Cassandra takes out Chutes and Ladders and lays it on the floor next to the cake. "While I beat you guys, we want to hear about what is going on," she says.

I set the pieces up in a row next to the start spot, and groan. "Let's just say the fact that I'm currently missing my sister's wedding does not seem that screwed up in comparison to how tragic my L.A. life has become."

Cassandra glances at Jake and then back at me. "What happened?"

I take a deep breath and for the next hour I fill them in on everything. The night of the awards, the breakup, Jordan and I in Tokyo. How terrible I feel about both of them, and their relationship with each other. It feels so good to finally let everything out, all the details.

"It's really too bad your sister is downstairs celebrating her wedding," Cassandra says when I pause to eat more cake. "Because this story has got to be worth more than ten grand."

Jake elbows her. "What she means to say is: are you okay?"

I look at him. People have asked me that so much. But somehow, hearing it from Jake, is the first time I feel like someone has actually wanted an honest answer. So I give him one.

"I don't know," I say. "I'm just trying to figure out what the new normal is. I keep thinking the answers will become clear, but every time I think I'm there, that I understand, I learn something about my new reality that brings me back to square one."

"And Rainer and Jordan?"

"No," I say, shaking my head. "It's not even about them—it's me. Sometimes it's hard to know who I am anymore. I'm not sure who to believe."

"Us," Cassandra says, no sarcasm.

"Well more than that, yourself," Jake says, eying Cassandra. "You can be a lot of different things at once." Jake's gaze shifts to me. "You can be the girl from Portland and the movie star. Life isn't stagnant—it's constantly evolving.

I mean look at the three of us. You and I once made out."

"Jake!" I say. I steal a quick glance at Cassandr. Her hand is over her mouth and her eyes are squeezed shut, laughing.

"It happened," he says. "And we're fine. But we couldn't have known that then."

"What's your point?"

"That life changes, and there are no guarantees. Sometimes all you can do is just what makes you happy right now, right in this moment."

"But what if what makes me happy now might end up making me miserable in the long run? How do I know?"

"You don't," Jake says. "There is no way to know what is coming. I go to a rally every weekend. I hope it's leading to a stop in global pollution and a ban on GMOs but I don't go for that day. I go for today. I go for the difference I can make along the way. And *that* makes me happy."

Cassandra has stopped laughing. She is looking at Jake with a mixture of curiosity and admiration that makes the back of my throat constrict.

"Stop worrying about what's *going* to happen and start thinking about what you're doing right *now*. Because whatever it is doesn't seem to be making you very happy."

"When did you get so smart?" I ask.

Jake smiles at Cassandra. "Somewhere around her," he says. He looks back at me. "All you can do is the best you can today. The rest, as they say, is out of our hands. You don't owe the world anything, Paige. I know you think you do, but you don't."

"There is so much I was wrong about," I say. "I screwed up."

"Join the club," Cassandra says. "We've all screwed up. Jake and I should have told you we were together. Your sister, Christ, should not have opened her big mouth." She waves her arms in the air. The big finish. "And Rainer and Jordan should have stopped letting anything and everything get in the way of their friendship." I open my mouth to retort, but Cassandra holds up her hand. "But we can't change that. All we can do is try and deal with, like Jake is saying, today."

"Today."

"Yeah," Cassandra says. "Today. So given what is, what do you want to do?"

I exhale. "Honestly," I say. "I want to dance with my best friends."

Cassandra laughs and scrunches up her nose. "That," she says, "can be arranged. Come on."

She drags Jake and I to our feet and we make our way downstairs. We eat some food and then the band starts playing old tunes—The Supremes and Michael Jackson— and we get on the dance floor. Jake twirls us both around and around and we spend the rest of the night like that— happy and full and dizzy. Together.

CHAPTER 15

"Paige? Are you there?"

Sandy's voice comes through the phone before I've managed to fully open my eyes. My head is still spinning from the champagne and sugar last night. I also don't think we got to bed until four AM. Cassandra is curled up next to me like a kitten and I move gently off the pillow, the phone still attached to my ear.

"Is everything okay?"

"I know you're supposed to be home through the week," she says. "But you need to come back to L.A. Alfonso wants to met with you and scheduling is super tight."

Alfonso is our new director. It's true, Wyatt is turning the franchise over. I've heard Alfonso is very by-the-book. Hard and fast with rules, nothing in a scene that's not in the script. I'm nervous.

"Now?"

"Today."

I survey the room—discarded Chutes and Ladders, clothes strewn everywhere, Jake asleep in my armchair.

"What time?" I ask.

"We're booking you on a three o'clock," Sandy says.

"What about Jordan and Rainer?"

Sandy pauses. "I'm not entirely sure where the three of you stand right now, but my advice would be to fix it fast. Alfonso isn't going to take kindly to all of this. Wyatt wouldn't have either. You guys used to be friends, right?"

I run a hand through my snarled hair. Friends. "Yeah," I say.

"Well that might be a good place to start," Sandy says. "Just pack yourself up and get to the airport."

Something occurs to me. *Closer to Heaven*. "Have we heard about the *Closer* audition?" I ask her.

Sandy sighs. "I think Billy left the project," she says. "I don't know where it's at right now. We're going to have to wait and see."

"I don't want to lose this."

"Cost of doing business, kid. Right now the price is getting your cute tush to the airport on time."

We hang up and Cassandra stirs. "What's going

on?" she asks. She rolls over and looks at the clock. "It's eight AM."

"I know," I whisper. "But I have to go back to L.A. today."

Cassandra sits up. She rubs her eyes. "Today? But you have another week here. We were going to do Nob Hill."

I come to sit down next to her. "I know, but I have to meet with the new director."

"This blows."

I nod. Jake snorts in the club chair, but his eyes don't open.

"Romance," Cassandra says.

"Hey, *you* ended up in bed with me."

She smiles a slow, sleepy smile. "I just got you back," she says.

"I know. Can you come visit?"

"Yeah, but Jake's not invited this time. Girl's trip."

"Definitely. And we still have Mexico," I point out.

Cassandra peels the covers down and stretches. "I'll understand if you can't make it."

"No way. I promise I'll be there. The movie can wait." But even as I say it, we both know it's not true. The movie can't wait. I can't make those kind of promises. Not now. Maybe not anymore.

Cassandra puts both of her hands on my shoulders. "Listen," she says. "I know we are living crazy different lives. And they're just going to get more different. But don't ever think that just because I don't know what it's like that I can't understand."

I pull her in for a hug, but she bounds off the bed. "Brush your teeth," she says. She crouches down next to Jake and kisses his cheek. "Rise and shine."

Jake stirs and murmurs something. "You have a protest in The Pearl in forty-five minutes, hotstuff," she says. "That community garden is not going to save itself."

Jake bolts upright. He rolls his neck and then stands and grabs Cassandra's hand. "We have to move," he says. "See ya, Pat."

I toss Cassandra's dress at her. She's wearing an old pair of boxer shorts and a T-shirt of mine. "Love you!" she calls over her shoulder.

I get dressed and go downstairs. Joanna and Bill left last night. My mom and dad are in the kitchen, sipping coffee.

"Hey," I say.

My mom looks up at me and winces. "Lower your voice," she says.

"Your mother is experiencing her second hangover in twenty-five years," my dad says, standing up and giving me his seat. "So you'll forgive her cheery attitude."

My mom smiles weakly at me.

"It was a great night," I tell her. "You did an amazing job."

She lifts a hand to her temple. "I think they liked it."

My dad hands me a cup of coffee and kisses my mom on the head. "They loved it," he says.

"I have bad news," I say.

Both parents look at me. "I have to go to back to L.A. this afternoon to meet with Alfonso. I just spoke to Sandy."

My mother nods. "I know, she called us."

"What?"

"Sandy used her telephone to call our telephone." My mother pantomimes. "Jeff is it one hundred degrees in here or is it just me?"

My father chuckles and takes off, presumably in pursuit of the thermostat or some ice water.

"She calls you?"

"Of course she calls me," my mom says. "I'm your mother."

"I didn't know."

My mom reaches out and gently grazes my cheek. "I know I said that stuff to you about coming home, but that's just because sometimes I want you here, where I can protect you. It's harder when you're out there—" She gestures out with her hand. "But I want you to know that just because I'm not there, doesn't mean I'm not doing what I can." She taps my nose with her index finger. "No matter how far away you are, I'm still always your mother."

I don't say anything—I just fold into her. "Ouch," she says. "Watch the head."

I pull back and raise my eyebrow. "I'm guessing Dad is going to drive me?"

My mom sits back and closes her eyes. "If he even so much as turns on that engine loudly, God help me, I'm getting a divorce."

Dad drops me off. "Take care of yourself," he says.

"I will."

"Don't let anyone tell you who you are, okay? You know all of that. Your mother taught you."

I smile at him. "You didn't do such a bad job, either."

"Maybe not," he says, hugging me close.

I wave goodbye as I go to check in. The airport is way less crowded than LAX and I board in relative peace. A few camera-phone pics, but at least I'm alone. I have the baseball hat I found in the Three Musketeers box yesterday on and I pull it down over my eyes the way I've gotten used to.

I sleep the whole way there. Cassandra kicks and Jake snores so last night was a wash and I'm exhausted. I only wake up when I feel the wheels hit the runway.

I go directly to meet with Alfonso the next morning. A car arrives to take me at eight AM. To my surprise and delight,

Alexis is there when I get to the studio. She's lounging in one of the studio exec's office.

"Paige," she says. "I'm sorry you got called back early."

"You too." I say. "Was Georgina upset?" I think about their plans for upfronts.

Alexis rolls her eyes. "She's back in love with Blake; she barely noticed I was there, let alone that I left." Alexis wraps her long arms around me. "Besides, I think you might need me right now more than she does."

"Hey, Paige." Maradith, the studio exec, waves from her desk. I let go of Alexis.

"Hey, how is it going?"

Maradith sighs. "I'm getting exercise tips from Twiggy over here. So you can imagine." She winks at me.

"It really is all about the core," Alexis says, employing a little more accent than usual and lifting up her sheer white tank top.

"Please put those away," I say. "I haven't even had coffee yet."

"That part we can fix," Maradith says. She calls in her assistant who comes back five minutes later, juggling Starbucks cups.

"Alfonso is waiting in the conference room," she says.

We take our cups and follow Maradith down the hall. She opens the door and I see Alfonso, and next to him, on either side, Jordan and Rainer.

"Paige," Alfonso says, rising and extending his hand. "It's a pleasure to meet you. Alexis, I don't think I've seen you since the *Mountain Rain* days."

Alexis beams.

"Please take a seat, ladies."

We sit. I can hear my heart hammering. *This is work*, I remind myself. *Be a goddamn professional.*

"I'm glad we're all here," Alfonso says. "I always like to meet together before we go on location. Just to get a feel for each other." Alfonso clasps his hands on the table. "I anticipate the dynamic being different on this film. We have a tight shoot. I just was telling the boys here—" he gestures on either side of him— "that we have less shooting days than we did for one, and more locations. So I'm really going to rely on you all to be present on set. Minimal distractions."

He doesn't look at any of us when he says it, but the implication hangs in the air.

Maradith is sitting next to us. "Alfonso was thinking that while we're all here, we could do our first read through."

I glance at Rainer. He looks up at me and gives me the slightest nod. "Sounds good to me," he says. "I don't have anywhere to be."

"Yeah, cool," Jordan says.

Maradith's assistant passes out scripts and then the

two of them depart, leaving Jordan, Rainer, Alexis and I alone with Alfonso.

We start reading. I fold back into August immediately. Or maybe it's not that I'm folding *back* into her, maybe it's that I'm letting her speak up. Maybe she's always there now. I used to feel unworthy of this role. Becoming August was something that took time and effort and a belief in myself and my own abilities that I wasn't sure I had. I used to think I didn't understand her. I used to think it made no sense—this over-dramatization of her choice. She's seventeen, for God's sake. But sitting at the table with both of them, reading our parts, I can't help but think that we're acting out something more than our roles.

Book two begins with August back home, with Ed. She's trying to figure out how to let go of Noah. To live without him. Ed wants to win her back, Maggie is acting out, and she isn't at all who she was when she left for the island.

We're doing this scene in August's kitchen with Ed, August and Maggie (Alexis). August begins to suspect that something might have happened with her boyfriend and her sister while she was on the island with Noah.

""I'm going to be sick." Alexis says. Maggie just caught Ed and August in the kitchen, kissing.

"Ever heard of knocking?" I ask, flipping the page.

Jordan makes a noise between a laugh and a snort. "Oh

come on," he says. "I know for a fact your stomach isn't that sensitive."

"If you're referring to the taco incident, then I have no comment." Alexis tosses Jordan a look.

"The taco incident?" I ask.

Jordan's eyebrows knit together. "It was nothing," he says.

"Tell me," I say, to Alexis.

"It wasn't a big deal," she says. "We just had some fun. You know, that thing we used to do before you—"

"Before I what?"

"Maggie . . ." Jordan's voice carries a warning.

"Before you came back and made him miserable again," she says.

Maggie is supposed to leave, and Alexis sits back in her chair.

"Don't listen to her," Jordan says to me. "She's just trying to make sense of all of this."

"So am I." I stop. I look at Jordan. "I feel like I came back and screwed everything up. Can I ask you something?"

"Always."

"Were you happier?" I say. "I mean, before you found me again?"

"Are you crazy?" Jordan asks. He's not just looking at his script, but glancing back and forth, up and down. Me and the page. "I couldn't breathe when you were gone. It was like my life stopped for those six weeks. I didn't even feel like I was alive."

Rainer shifts in his seat next to Jordan.

"What did Maggie mean, then?" I ask. I play with the edge of my script. I can feel my face is hot.

"We all love you," Jordan says. "It's hard to go through losing someone you love. She thought she'd never get you back. You just need to give her time, that's all. We all just need time."

We keep reading. We're almost through when Maradith pokes her head in.

"Sorry to interrupt you, guys, but I need Alfonso."

"Alright, we just about made it," he says.

I feel disoriented, like I'm coming out of a dream. I blink and see Jordan is looking at me.

"Never met a cast with more chemistry," Alfonso tells us. "The next time I'll see you all will be in Hawaii."

"Alfonso is flying out tomorrow," Maradith says, snatching up her Starbucks cup. "I believe you're all arriving the week after next?"

"Yeah except for this one," Jordan says, gesturing to Alexis.

"I have to stay for the Do Something event I'm chairing," Alexis says proudly. "You guys are Skyping in, by the way." She turns to me. "And I'm dropping off a T-shirt later today. I want you to Insta yourself in it."

"She doesn't have Instagram," Rainer says.

"Yes she does," Alexis shoots back.

Rainer looks at me. I shrug. "She set it up," I say. "I don't really know how it works."

"Okay," Alfonso says, clearly having had enough of our social media banter. "I'll see you all soon. Get ready to work."

Rainer shakes Alfonso's hand. "We're really looking forward to it."

"Seconded," Alexis says. She stands as well.

Alfonso follows Maradith out the door. "We're sending a car for you guys," she says. "But feel free to stay or order lunch. Ella can help with whatever." She gestures outside, to where her assistant is. "We're excited!"

The door snaps shuts behind her and then silence fills the space.

"I wonder what we could steal here," Alexis fills in.

Rainer laughs. "No cash. But the good booze is hidden in the next conference room." He gestures with his thumb.

I think about how many times Rainer has been in these offices. I wonder where his father is and if Rainer has seen him in the last month. There is so much I don't know about his life anymore.

"I should head back," Jordan says, standing. "I'll see you guys on Maui."

Alexis makes a move for the door. "Can I hitch a ride?

Brit dropped me off and took the car." Alexis glances at me. "Sorry," she says. "We're just . . ."

I wave my hand through the air. "I'll call you later," I say.

Jordan holds the door open for Alexis and then they disappear into the hallway, leaving me alone with Rainer.

"Do you want to have lunch?" he asks me.

My stomach is rumbling. I didn't have breakfast this morning, or dinner last night, which puts my last meal at a piece of leftover cake at my parents' house. But all of that takes a backseat to the fact that Rainer is asking to spend time with me, something he hasn't done since before the movie awards.

"Yeah," I say. "I'm starving."

"Cool."

Rainer follows me out of the conference room, down the elevator and to the parking lot. He holds the door to his familiar Range Rover open for me.

"Where do you feel like going?" he asks as he starts driving.

I shrug. "Somewhere we won't be recognized."

"You got it."

We drive through In N Out Burger. Rainer gets a protein-style cheeseburger and I do the same. We agree on fries. "We'll share them," I say when Rainer points out we have to be half naked in front of cameras in a few short weeks.

We eat in the parking lot. I inhale mine in three minutes flat. The burgers are delicious. It seems crazy, that after all this time in L.A., I've never had one.

"Thanks for feeding me," I say.

"No problem." He looks over at me. "Home, then?"

I nod. I want to say something else to him. To tell him . . . what, exactly? That it feels nice being here with him? That I'm sorry? That I hope he can, at some point, get to a point where he can trust me again?

What I end up saying is: "Can we go back to Bel Air and just hang out for a little while?"

"Yeah," he says. "I'd like that."

CHAPTER 16

We turn off Sunset and weave our way up to the house. There are no photographers anywhere in sight as we pull through the gate and down to the car park. Rainer comes around, opens my door, and helps me down.

The house looks the same and I feel a rush of affection wash over me as I think about how we lived together here. I wonder if he's changed things since I moved out, if the living room is reconfigured. Once I open the door, though, I see that it's all the same. Nothing has changed. That is, besides the fact that Britney Nichols, Rainer's ex, is seated on his couch.

"What are you doing here?" I say automatically. My eyes jump from Britney, perched on the sofa, to Rainer, standing behind me, but he looks just as clueless as I feel.

"I thought we could spend some quality time together today, Rain." She dangles a key from her pointer finger. "The gate was open, and you still keep it under the mat. I guess some things don't change."

Rainer closes the door and stands firmly, arms crossed. "Now is not a good time."

"According to Alexis, and *the universe*," Britney rolls her eyes. "You two broke up. My mistake."

"What do you want?" I ask her.

Britney laughs. A childish, girly laugh that makes my insides feel like rotting fruit. "Your boyfriend is my friend," she says. "He didn't tell you we've been spending time together?"

I glance at Rainer, who is shifting uncomfortably from foot to foot. "Not like that," he says.

"Oh, no," Britney says, in mock-sincerity. "We're just *friends*. You know, kind of like you and Jordan?"

"Enough," Rainer says. "Britney, you need to leave. Now."

"Just a little while longer," Britney says, tossing her feet up. "It's so rare I get to have a heart to heart with Paige."

I snort. Rainer takes a stride towards the couch. "Britney, come on. Not now."

"No, I think now," Britney says. "Rainer, I'm sorry, but your girl deserves to know the truth."

"Truth about what?"

"Britney," Rainer says through gritted teeth, "I'm going to ask you one last time to leave."

Britney walks silently over to Rainer. She touches his jaw with her hand and my eyes widen as his narrow at her.

"Paige," Britney says, her hand still on Rainer. "Why don't you decide? Do you want to know the real story about you and Rainer? Or should I leave?"

"What are you talking about?" I say. My voice is shaking. Something about the way Rainer is looking at her, wild-eyed, makes my feet feel like they've grown roots. I can't move.

Britney turns her attention from him to me. She reminds me of a mountain lion, the way she moves. Like at any moment, she could pounce.

"It was cute, wasn't it?" she says. "The way you and Rain got together? He fell in love with you in Hawaii. The brightest rising star in Hollywood besotted with some average teenage girl."

"Stop!" Rainer yells.

"What's your point?" I say.

Her eyes flash. "You never wondered?"

"Wondered *what*?"

"Let me spell it out for you, sweetheart." She's almost to me. I can smell her perfume. Tangy sweet. "Rainer didn't fall in love with you. His dear old daddy told him to date

232

you, and he simply followed orders."

I almost laugh. "You must be kidding."

Britney doesn't say anything. She just looks at me, unblinking.

"You really expect me to fall for that?"

"He pursued you until you said yes, right?" Britney says. "Curious timing, wasn't it? That he wanted you to be with him right before the big premiere?"

"How do you . . ."

Britney runs a hand over her hair. "I think at this point, PG, you're the only one who doesn't know."

I think about our first weeks on Maui. How Rainer was immediately there for me. How he made it the point of his whole day to make sure I felt safe and happy and *good*. I think about how he pursued me after that. How I wasn't sure if we were just friends until he made it clear— he wanted to be with me.

But what if . . .

What if Greg spoke to him before we started filming? What if he told him that the more press a couple gets, the better?

"Why are you telling me this?" I ask.

Britney's eyes flash. "I'd want to know," she says. "If I were you."

"Britney," Rainer says. "Go."

"Fine by me," she says, picking up her purse. "I'll leave

233

you two to your history. It seems to be all you have left anymore."

When she's gone, I turn to Rainer. He's looking at the floor. "Did your dad . . ." I can barely get the words out. "Did your dad tell you to date me?"

He just shakes his head.

I feel my blood pressure rising. "Tell me," I say again. "You asked me to be honest with you and I was. Rainer, did your dad tell you to date me?"

He looks at me then and I know, heartbreakingly, and with absolute certainty, the answer to my question.

"Oh my God," I say. "This whole time."

Rainer shakes his head. He makes a move towards me, to grab my arm, but I shake him off.

"Fuck," he says. "No. Paige—"

"Yes!"

"No. Paige, listen to me."

I feel like someone else, like I'm playing a part. Some crazy movie star engaged in an affair in the Hollywood Hills. I feel like I should have a long cigarette in one hand and a martini in the other. "What could you possibly have to say?"

I'm fighting through the fog. The images of us on the island. Late nights. Running lines. Our trip to Paia. Dinners at Longhi's. Our promises to one another. It was all a lie.

"Please," he says. "Please, you just have to let me

explain." Rainer runs a hand through his hair. He takes a step towards me. I take one back.

"I can't believe this," I say. "I can't—"

"Paige . . ." His voice is pleading.

"I trusted you," I say. "I built a life around you. I *chose* you."

At this Rainer throws his hands up. "Jesus does everything have to be about Jordan?"

"Jordan?" I look at him, incredulous. "Do you even care? Did you *ever* care? Or was that all part of the stunt. Act like the jilted boyfriend . . ." I trail off. My fists are clenched by my sides. "After everything we've been through. Did you ever even . . ."

"Love you?" Rainer shakes his head. "Yes, of course I love you."

There it is again: love. It makes me stop. It makes him stop, too. We look at each other over a divide that all at once seems impossibly long and equally short. And I know we're both thinking the same thing, both aware of it hanging between us—whether it's going to hammer us in or split us apart.

Rainer goes to sit down on the couch. He puts his head in his hands. "Sit down," he says. I do.

He pauses, and then he begins. "I liked you immediately," he says, softly. "You were warm and unaware and so naïve. You were so pure and I wanted—I wanted to be your friend. But then—" He exhales. "Then my dad told me it would be great for the franchise if we were dating. He told me it would extend the fantasy. He said to get to know you, that's all, and see how I felt."

I don't move. It feels like my whole body has turned to lead.

"But then I did and—" He clears his throat. "I fell in love with you."

"Rainer . . ."

"It's *true*, Paige. When I asked you to be mine on Maui, I meant it. I wasn't pretending. Think about everything that has happened. Do you really think it was all a lie?"

"I don't know what to think." Nothing is real. Nothing is the way it seems. These last few months, it has felt like I've been struggling to not just be an amalgamation of the stories written about me. But turns out, I didn't even know the truth at the center of my own life.

Rainer was the one grounding thing I had. The one person I could count on through all of this. He was the only thing that felt, really and truly, *real*. And now I know all we were doing was playing pretend, just like our characters. In love, in front of the world. "I have to go," I say. I push past him.

"Stop." He reaches for me. "Stay, let's talk about this."

"I don't want to talk," I say, moving now towards the door. "I just want to be alone."

I suddenly remember I don't have a car here. I stand in the doorway, Rainer behind me.

"I have to call a cab," I say.

I spin to look at Rainer. I expect him to launch into another pleading speech, but he must read something on my face, because instead he goes to the bowl on the counter and plucks the Range Rover keys.

"Here," he says. "Take the car. I'll have Sandy pick it up tomorrow."

I take them from him wordlessly.

"Paige, I'm so sorry," he says. "Whatever I can do to make this right, I will. Please just tell me."

I look at him. His beautiful face is tear-streaked.

"I don't know," I say. "That's the problem."

I drive home in a daze. I park in the back, go in through the courtyard, and unlock the door. I plop down on the couch, my head in my hands. My thoughts are spinning too fast for me to keep up. I'm just about to head upstairs when I hear a knock at the window. I look through the glass, and see Jordan waving from the other side

"What are you doing here?" I say when I pull open the door.

"Alexis asked me to drop this off for her." He holds up a bag. I take a step towards him and pluck it out of his hands. It's the Do Something T-shirt and an iPhone. For Instagramming, right. "Also, your courtyard lock is kind of lame. You may want to look into that." He gives me a small lopsided smile.

"Well thanks," I say. "I could have picked it up."

Jordan shrugs. "You know Alexis—patience isn't really her strong suit."

"Yeah."

"Anyway I'll just . . . Are you okay?" He's looking at my face and I see his train of thought veer off into concern.

"Fine," I say. I retreat, but Jordan follows me inside.

"You don't sound fine. What's going on?" Jordan takes the bag out of my hands and places it on the sofa. "Talk to me."

I shake my head. "Rainer lied to me," I say. "His dad told him to date me. They set the whole thing up."

"Jesus," he says. "How did you—?"

"Britney just told me everything, and Rainer didn't deny it." I blink at him. "It wasn't even real."

Jordan looks at me. His gaze is measured. "Do you really believe that?"

"He admitted it!"

Jordan shakes his head. "About it not being real. Come on, Paige, he loves you. We both know that."

"You're taking his side? Jordan, just go." I put my hands over my eyes. They burn with tears.

But Jordan doesn't leave. Instead he places his arms around me and wraps me up in a hug. I bury my face in the cool cotton of his T-shirt. I breathe him in. He smells like he always does—like dirt and sea. Like Hawaii. And then, suddenly, it hits me. The realization makes my insides feel hot and sticky: Jordan isn't surprised.

The past begins to sort itself out, like a magic wand has been waved, returning a disorderly room to its rightful state. I can see everything clearly. That fight Jordan and Greg had before the premiere. It was about this. Jordan knew what Greg had done and they were fighting about me.

I pull back. "You knew."

Jordan stays perfectly still.

"You knew and you never told me."

"I didn't know," he says, releasing me. "I suspected, at first. I know Greg. But then—"

"Do you have any idea how different everything would have been? That press conference never would have happened. I wouldn't have chosen Rainer. We could have been together, Jordan."

Jordan looks at me like I'm crazy. "And then what? You would have been with me by default? Excuse me if that doesn't sound all that appealing, Paige."

I just gape at him. "What would it have mattered if we were together?"

"Because," he says, throwing his hands up. "I don't want to be your second choice. I don't want to be the guy you're with because things didn't work out with Rainer. I don't want to be your back up."

"You're not—" I start, but I can't continue. It's too much, all of it. "I can't do this anymore," I say.

Jordan nods. "Right there with you."

We stand fuming at each other.

"I'm sorry for what happened in Tokyo," Jordan continues. "I shouldn't have put you in that position."

"You're *sorry*?"

"Yeah," he says. "I am." He looks at me and I see it all written there beneath the anger—a million regrets, none of which we know how to fix. "See you on set," he says. Then he pulls open the door and is gone.

CHAPTER 17

The next two weeks are comprised of non-stop meetings, photo shoots, and personal training sessions that remind me of Joanna's labor. I barely have time to crash before Sandy is calling me again. All for *Locked*. *Closer to Heaven* seems farther than it ever has. Sandy tells me it's time to let it go, that I need to focus on all we have coming up, but like many things in my life it's proving to be easier said than done.

I'm at Alexis's, the night before I am due to fly out, watching her throw tissue paper and bathing-suit bottoms around the living-room floor. I don't think she's quite gotten it that we're going to Hawaii, but not on vacation. She's just gone shopping for me and is now demanding I pack at her house, where she can supervise. "Plus," she said, "You'll clearly need to borrow everything."

"See? I told you you could mix separates," she says. She holds up a red string thing and black bottom? Top? It's hard to tell.

"Don't you do enough shopping for yourself?" I ask her. "Why do you have to start in with me?"

"Because you don't," she says.

"I wish you were coming tomorrow," I say.

Alexis nods. "It's only a week, though. And we're gonna see each other on Skype!"

"True."

She throws a white dress towards the suitcase and tosses her arms overhead when it makes it in. "And then I will be there to help your angst-ridden behind."

"I am not angst ridden," I say, scooping up a wedge.

"Yes, darling, you are." She looks at me funny for a moment and then starts folding some bedazzled denim shorts. "Do you want to come out tonight?" she asks. "Georgina is throwing a soiree at the beach."

A party at Georgina's actually sounds kind of fun. Plus I could use seeing some other faces before the three of us take off for Triangle, Part Two.

"Sure."

"Fabulous. We're going to do a barbeque. Just us, plus Tailor." She makes a face at me.

"She's not so bad," I say.

"That is not an opinion I share." Alexis stands and goes to her closet. She pulls out a blue dress. "Yes?"

I'm just about to tell her no when I hear the front door open. Immediately, I see Alexis freeze. "Shit," she says.

I look behind me to where her gaze is fixed. There is Britney, standing in the entryway.

Instantly, I'm filled with rage. All the emotions from her attack at Rainer's come to the surface. I'm ready to spew.

"You have got to be kidding me," Britney says. She has a Whole Foods bag tucked under her arm and she drops it on the counter.

"I thought you were seeing Sebastian this afternoon," Alexis says. "And you were coming home later?"

Britney doesn't take her eyes off me. "He moved our session to earlier."

I take in her Lululemon-clad frame. Her hair is up in a messy ponytail.

"Home?" I say. "Is she living here now?"

"What do you care?" Britney asks.

I throw my hands up. "I'm out of here," I say. I rock myself back onto my heels and stand. I go into the bedroom to grab the rest of the shopping bags. Alexis follows me.

"Sorry," she says. "I didn't think she was going to be back this early. She's just been crashing with me for a little while."

I grab the Kitson bag and drop a sweater that's trailing on the floor inside another one from Reiss. "It's fine," I say. "She's your friend."

"She doesn't have anyone right now," Alexis continues. "She's . . ."

I look at Alexis. I can see something written there, but I don't know how to read it.

"She did this to herself," I say, pushing on. "You should have seen how she told me about Rainer. She was *delighted*. She couldn't have been happier to make me miserable."

Alexis eyes me. "I know, I know. You've told me ten times, but she's been through a lot. She's not a bad person. She's—"

I grab the last bag and toss the tissue paper on the floor a little too aggressively. "Not a very good one, either? I'm sorry, Alexis, but that girl has been straight-up trouble in everyone's lives. I don't know why you can't see that."

"Don't hold back."

I look up to see Britney in the doorway. "You destroyed my relationship," I say. "I hope you're happy."

"I didn't destroy anything," Britney says. "It was broken way before I came along. All I did was tell you the truth."

I drop the bags to the floor. I hear them rustle against each other. "Why do you hate me so much? What did I ever do to you? It's not my fault that Jordan wanted—"

"You?" Britney laughs. "Please, you think I care?"

"Jordan told me about how you went to him that night," I say. "He told me you kissed him."

Britney's eyes flash. "God, you're young," she says. "I didn't want Jordan. I kissed him—so what? You've never gotten lost in a moment?" She looks at me and it's like she's seeing *my* moments with Jordan. That day on the beach, our night in Tokyo. "It didn't mean anything," she finishes. "It was always Rainer."

"So that's why you told me?" I say. "To get him back all for yourself? Even if it meant hurting him?"

"Hurting *him*?" Britney stares at me. "Do you have any idea what I've been through? Do you have any idea what it's like to be assaulted by the father of the man that you love?"

"Okay." Alexis steps in between us and holds her hand up. "Let's take this down a notch." She looks helplessly at me but my eyes are fixed on Britney. All of a sudden, my blood has run cold. I hear every sound, like my senses are on hyper alert. The next door neighbors' lawnmower, traffic moving outside.

"No," I say. "I don't."

Britney just stands there. She looks broken.

"I'm sorry Greg did that to you," I say.

Some hair falls into her face, but she doesn't tuck it back. "I saw the way you looked at me at the MTV awards," she says, her voice just a register softer now. "And I know what you think of me. I don't need your pity. I know you hate me."

I shake my head. "No," I say. "I don't hate you." Is that true? It feels true. "I think you've been in a lot of pain," I continue. "I didn't really know how it could feel—the press, the lies, all of it—until it happened to me, too."

"It's not the same thing."

"You're right," I say. "It's not."

Whatever happened to me, it's a million times worse what happened to her. I *chose* to call Jordan. I *chose* to let my feelings take over. But Britney? Britney didn't choose any of it. Not what happened, not how the story came out, certainly not its lasting impact. She was a victim. We both wanted the same thing: the chance to write our own story. But I've been doing exactly what the press has to both of us—I've been filling it in for her, and it hasn't been fair.

Britney sucks in her bottom lip. The gesture feels oddly vulnerable from her. "Greg told Rainer to date you," she says.

"Yeah," I say. "You mentioned that."

"But that's not why he's with you." She blinks and looks away. Alexis shifts next to us. "He loves you," she says.

I feel my heart catch in my throat. I can't think what to say but the truth. "I love him too," I whisper.

No one speaks for a moment, and then Alexis steps in. "Brit," she says gently, "maybe we should head down to Georgina's."

Britney nods and turns to leave the bedroom, but I stop her.

"I want to start over," I say. "I think we both made a lot of assumptions. I'd like to change that." She looks back at me and for a moment our eyes lock. I see something familiar in them. Something that reminds me a lot of myself.

"There's no such thing as starting over," she says. Then she leaves the room. I hear the door open and close behind her.

CHAPTER 18

Britney is right. There is no such thing as starting over. But going back to Hawaii, landing and breathing that clean air and feeling the faint smell of plumeria and the soft island breeze, makes me think that maybe the way you move forward is to go home.

Because as soon as I make my way groggily off the plane and down the corridor and through the sliding glass doors to outside and the air hits me, I feel it. I feel like I'm home.

The night smells like flowers and sea salt—a mix that is somehow invigorating and peaceful, all at once.

No one here notices me. Or at least, they don't care. I take my hat off and shake my hair out. I hike my carry-on higher on my shoulder and take the familiar route out to the left and down the stairs to baggage claim.

I stop on the landing and look below me, expecting to see a driver that Sandy said she would arrange. But instead I see Rainer.

He looks a little tired but I know it's something only I can see. He's still his usual movie-star stunning, and he's holding a sign that says **PG** in big, pink magic marker.

I walk the stairs slowly. When I get to him, I pause. "I thought they were sending a car," I say.

He shrugs. "Didn't feel like the right welcome."

We look at each other, the night air cooling around us.

"Should we get your bags?"

"Yeah thanks."

We go over to the carousel. I just have one duffle, packed to the brim with things I'm sure will ultimately end up in Alexis's room.

I point it out to Rainer and he slings it over his shoulder. "After you," he says.

The Maui airport is open and as we cross over to the parking lot, to Rainer's neon-blue cruiser, I look up to see the palm trees swaying and the stars sparkling above us. It's almost enough for me to forget where Rainer and I are, what has happened. Almost.

"It hasn't changed," I whisper.

"No," Rainer says. "It hasn't."

But we have. We drive in silence with the top down.

The familiar landscape waxes and wanes around us. I can't wait to see everything in the light of day tomorrow.

We pull up to the condos. We rented the same ones as last time. Right in Wailea, right by the ocean.

Our keys are at the front desk, along with a way-too-big flower bouquet from Amanda. "Would you like us to bring it to your room?" the desk girl asks.

"No," I say. "They're yours."

We make our way to my room, Rainer still hauling the suitcase behind me. He stops at the door and I pull out the key, sliding it in and waiting for the click. He follows me inside.

"Where should I drop this?" he asks.

"Anywhere," I say. "It doesn't matter."

I take it in. The bedroom is to the right and then the hallway spills into the living room and beyond that, the balcony. The shades are up and the sliding doors have been opened, allowing for the most delicious trade breeze. My feet on the hardwood floor feel cool and steady.

Rainer puts the bag in the bedroom and then comes and stands next to me.

There are so many memories here. Morning coffee on the terrace, ordering sushi, running lines on the sofa. I think of the two of us, how good we were. Or how good we seemed.

I feel Rainer's hand reach out and touch me lightly

between my shoulder blades. "I need to say something," he tells me.

"I know," I say. "But I need to say something first." I step back from his reach and over to the couch. He follows.

"Okay," he says. "Of course."

I cross my feet underneath me. Rainer puts a hand on the back of the couch. I take a deep breath. "Rainer, I know what we had was real—I'm not an idiot. I was there, too. I know you love me, just like I love you." I see relief in his eyes. It shines so bright I think they might blow a fuse. "But it doesn't change what happened. You lied to me. You came after me not because of how you felt but because of orders you were given. What does it say about us, our relationship, that you couldn't even be honest with me?"

"I didn't think it mattered," Rainer says. "Who cares how we got together if we're together now?"

"Because," I say. "Our life isn't pretend. We're not chess pieces to be moved around at the world's will. I don't want my private life to be some kind of public fantasy."

"It's not. *We're* not."

"I think we are. Being with you made me feel protected, but it also made me feel scared. And I'm not saying this to hurt you, but it's the truth. It's so much. It's too much, Rainer. Sometimes being with you, being that couple, made me feel like I didn't know who I was."

Rainer runs his palm up and down the back of the sofa.

"These last few months, away from you—it's been scary but it has also felt good. I want to be able to do stuff on my own and not feel like I need you by my side. I don't want us to be together because we *need* each other. I want us to be together because we *want* each other. As Rainer and Paige, not Noah and August."

Rainer nods. He doesn't say anything.

"I haven't been fair to you," I say. "I punished you for keeping me at an arm's length and not thinking I could handle things when I gave you no reason to believe I could. I took no responsibility for myself. I left it all up to you. I don't want to be that girl anymore."

I get quiet and Rainer's eyes study my face. "Can I say something now?" he asks.

I nod.

"I was wrong," he says. "But not for following my dad's advice. Honestly, Paige, telling me to go after you might have been the one good thing my father has ever done. I was wrong to think you had to be protected. I've just seen fame destroy people. And I didn't want you to end up like Britney. I didn't want you to fall and not have me there to catch you." Rainer swallows. "But you're stronger than I gave you credit for. I want you to be. What kind of guy would I be if I didn't want you to be everything you are? Look, Paige, I don't want to make this harder for you. If you say we're done, then that's your choice, and I'll respect it. But I also need you to know I haven't taken myself out of the running."

I look up at him. His blue eyes are so clear and bright. The hope stings me. Burns me right at the heart.

"I still want to be with you," he says simply. "Now, on our terms. I just need you to know that."

He looks down at me and smiles. That dazzling, megawatt, movie-star smile. And then he kisses me. It happens in a split second. Blink, his lips are on mine.

It has been so long since we've kissed, but I remember him perfectly. He's so familiar to me here, now—back on Maui, where we know how to be together. My body remembers him. He presses a hand gently against the back of my head, tangles his fingers in my hair. And then, just as quickly as he began, he pulls back, touching his forehead to mine. "There is a lot of good here," he says. I feel his breath on my cheek. His eyelashes tickle my face.

"I know," I whisper.

I think about that advice people are always giving out—*follow your heart*. What they forget to tell you is that your heart can want many things at once. It can want love and romance and friendship all at the same time. It can feel betrayed and compelled. It can feel swollen and broken. Our hearts are big. There is room in there to hold a lot. There is room in there to hold two people.

*

We don't waste any time getting started on rehearsals. Late nights, early mornings. Working with green screens and harnesses and animatronic plants. This is what our training was for, but it's still a steep learning curve here, on set. We're suspended from ropes fifty feet in the air. It's terrifying, but pretty awesome. Our stunts in *Locked* seemed massive, but like any good franchise, they just keep upping the stakes.

Alfonso is exacting. There is no room for mistakes. Every second is scheduled. Wyatt was passionate, incredibly demanding, but Alfonso's method is totally different. He gives us more free reign. He doesn't talk through scenes with us, he just expects us to know. Some of the time, we do, but other times I find myself missing Wyatt's direction. Even if more often than not he was screaming it.

I can tell Rainer and Jordan feel it, too.

The three of us are trying our best, but to me we feel like planets orbiting around each other, never fully coming in contact. Alfonso encourages what he calls a "spotlessly professional" atmosphere, so for the most part, the tension goes unnoticed, played off to method acting on the part of Ed and Noah.

We're rehearsing a fight scene four days in. Ed and Noah are having it out. It's a scene from later in the book, almost at the end, but we're shooting it early. Alfonso is with us on the sound stage, and Jessica stands next to him.

I figured she would follow Wyatt on to his next project, but she's back with us. When I asked her about it, she shrugged and said it felt like something she needed to see through. It's nice to have her here. It makes things on set feel way more normal.

"I trusted you," Jordan says. "And you betrayed me."

"You betrayed me years ago, Ed," Rainer says. "When you told me I shouldn't be with her, that it had to be you. I listened to you. And all along all you had were your own interests at heart."

"No," Jordan says. "I had hers."

The press loves to talk about how real life is imitating fiction, how we've become our characters, stuck in this love triangle. I think, in a strange way, we've believed it, too. Rainer wasn't the only one who went in search of real life to imitate fiction. We're all guilty of it.

On the first movie, I was afraid of not being able to be August. After *Locked* came out, I was afraid of not being about to be Paige, the Movie Star. To live up to everyone's expectations. But standing here watching them I begin to see that we've been drinking way too much Kool Aid. We're not our characters. Jordan isn't Ed and Rainer isn't Noah. Not even close.

And perhaps most importantly, I'm not August.

I'm Paige Townsen. And I'm not choosing between Rainer and Jordan for the rest of my life, because I'm eighteen. I'm not supernatural, I'm *human*. And most likely I will fall in love again, maybe even a few times. August thinks that the choice between Ed and Noah is the last one she'll ever make. It's forever. But this isn't about forever. Jake was right—it's about *now*. And right now I don't want this fiction to be our reality. Not anymore.

Alfonso calls break and Jordan goes to grab his phone. I see him looking at Rainer and I, and then he jogs over.

"Hey, we have to get on Skype," he says.

Rainer swigs some water out of a Save the Whales jug Jake gave him. "What?"

"Alexis is doing that school visit for Do Something," I remind him. "We told her we'd join in."

"Oh right," Rainer says. "What's she doing with them again?"

"Ambassador for bullying," Jordan says.

"Fine," Rainer says, more to me. His tone is frayed, and I feel my pulse lurch. The last thing we need is a fight before we have to video broadcast ourselves to millions of people.

"Come on," I say. "We made a promise."

"The three of us?" Rainer asks.

Jordan glances at me. "Yeah. It's only ten minutes."

Rainer snaps closed the top of his water bottle. "For Alexis, sure."

I follow them back up to the condos, but instead of making a left when we get to the lobby, we make a right.

I've never been on this side of the condos before. I've never been to Jordan's room before.

He leads us up a side staircase and then around to the left. He pops the door open and I walk in, Rainer behind.

Jordan's condo faces half out to the water, and half to the mountain. You can see all the way up the hills here—hills that I know disappear into Haleakala.

Rainer flops himself down on the couch. Jordan switches on his laptop. I take a seat on the coffee table, across from them.

"I'm dialing in," Jordan says.

They both look right at me.

"Okay," I say.

"Okay," Rainer says, shaking his head. He gestures to the space between him and Jordan. "You're probably going to need to come sit here."

I smooth down my hair. "Yeah," I say. "Sure." I take a seat. The couch isn't giant, and my knee brushes Jordan's. I put my hands on my thighs and keep them there.

The screen shows the three of us. I look down at the little box with our picture and then a woman's face appears.

"Oh my goodness," she says. "You're never going to believe who just came to join us."

She steps back to reveal a fully packed auditorium and the kids go wild. Whooping and screaming.

"We're calling you from Hawaii," Rainer says. He

waves and slings an arm over the back of the couch. "We miss you, Alexis!"

Alexis is standing at a podium on the stage, wearing the T-shirt she gave me but altered in such a way that it looks wildly flattering on her. She waves at us. "Hey, friends!"

"How is it going?" Jordan asks. I see her beam back at him. "We can't wait for you to get here."

"Is anyone else jealous these guys have spent all day on the beach?" Alexis asks the students.

"We're working," I say.

Alexis winks at me. "You guys want to hang out while I talk?"

More yelling. Rainer leans forward. "We'll stick around if you guys stop screaming!"

The students freak out even more, and I'm reminded of the impact Rainer has on people. Even here, in Jordan's living room, from thousands of miles away, he has command of the audience.

"Do your thing," I say. "We're not going anywhere."

Alexis looks at us and out of the corner of my eye I catch Jordan give her a quick thumbs up. She takes a deep breath. Even on the screen I can feel her energy. She seems nervous. I've never seen Alexis nervous before.

"I'm here today to talk about bullying. I joined with Do Something about six months ago and I had planned to speak today, as I have many times before, about kindness in schools and treating each other with respect. I was going to tell you about how it gets better after high school and I want to be clear all of that is true . . . but there's something I need to say first."

Confused, I look at Jordan, but his eyes are fixed to the screen.

"I'm gay," Alexis says.

I blink, and feel Rainer shift next to me. I know they're watching us—not just the students, but the world—and that this clip will be everywhere. I can't react with surprise, which might register as unkindness. And I could never be unkind to Alexis, who now I realize is braver and more selfless than I ever knew before.

She looks down at the podium and I see her brush the back of her hand against her face. I want to reach through the screen and hold her. Stand with her. I know now why she wanted us to call in. She wanted us to be here and that fact alone makes me feel the most intense, true love for her.

Alexis inhales, ready to continue, except she is silenced. Because the entire auditorium has broken out into a chorus of shouts and cheers and applause. It is more deafening than anything I have heard before. Louder than our premiere. But it doesn't feel scary or burdensome or panic-inducing. This collective expression feels like love. And I know Alexis feels it too because all at once her head is up and she is beaming.

"Yeah," she says, nodding. "I'm a gay woman." More screaming. It sounds so freaking beautiful I start doing it myself.

"Thank you," she says. She holds up her hand for people to quiet down. "I wasn't going to say anything. I wasn't sure I was ever going to come out. I live my life in such a public way, and frankly, I don't think my sexuality is anyone's business. It doesn't affect my job."

People are clapping maniacally.

"But." Alexis holds up her hand and tosses her hair. She's back working the crowd. "I realized that I was starting to live a lie. And I don't want any of you to think there is anything wrong with being, openly and proudly, who you are."

At this people go nuts. Rainer and Jordan next to me are whooping and clapping. I find that I have tears rolling down my face.

"These are my friends," Alexis says. "And I guarantee you it does not make one single difference to them who I decide to date."

She looks at us and Rainer leans forward. "Not true," he tells her through the screen. "We do care, because we want you to be happy. And, Alexis? Goddamn, we're proud."

I look at Jordan. He has tears in his eyes. "I love you, A," he says.

"Back at you, babe."

Even though we're on Skype, and through a screen, I know she's looking right at me. She has been so brave. And I can't help but think, as she cocks an eyebrow at me, that she's challenging me to be the same.

I blow her a kiss. She turns back to the auditorium. And then she keeps speaking. She talks about truth and integrity, and kindness. And leading with your heart—no matter how "off the path" it may take you.

"The thing about life," she says, "is that sometimes the roads that seem impossible just have some rocks in your way. They're not boulders, they're just rocks. You can move them. You are strong enough." She finishes with this: "I will help you lift them."

We hang up with promises of seeing her soon. The last thing I see is Alexis being enveloped into a huge hug by students.

Once we close the computer the three of us are quiet. No one moves. And I suddenly realize it's not their job to say anything, it's mine. Alexis stood up in front of the world and told us who she is. She spoke her truth. Now it's my turn.

I flip myself around to the coffee table so I'm facing them. Jordan is looking at the floor, but Rainer is looking right at me.

"She's amazing," I say.

They both nod.

"She had mentioned she might—" Jordan says. "Pretty epic."

"How long have you known?" I ask Jordan.

He shrugs. "Forever, I guess." He looks at me. "I still had a thing for her, though."

To my complete surprise, Rainer laughs. I see the slight edge of a smile on Jordan's lips, too.

"I have to tell you guys something," I say.

Rainer sits back and crosses a foot over his leg. Jordan is still avoiding my gaze.

"I know I've been selfish, inexcusably so. You were right, Rainer. This isn't fair. And I'm so sorry for what I've put you both through." I take a deep breath. I just say it. "Which is why I won't choose."

At this Rainer and Jordan both look at me. What I see there is a mix of so many emotions it makes me feel dizzy. "If it means giving one of you up, and you giving up each other, then I won't do it."

I see Jordan look up at Rainer and then fall silent again. Rainer leans forward. "Paige," he says, gently. "No one is going anywhere."

"That's not true," I say. "This whole thing—" I gesture around me, to the space between us— "Isn't how it should be. I don't want things to be awkward and miserable between the two of you. It's my fault that—"

Rainer shakes his head. "It's not your fault," he says. But you also can't expect things to just return to normal. That's not the way life works."

"What would normal even be?" I ask. I have no idea anymore. Nothing is the way it used to be, least of all me. I'm not Paige Townsen, employee of Trinkets N Things. I'm Paige Townsen, star of *Locked*. And I love both of these boys. In ways that are different and the same, all at once. Standing in that audition room last year I never would have thought my life could change this much. But that's just the thing—it has. For better or worse this is where I am. But where I'm going is something I'm not sure I'm ready to face yet.

Rainer exhales. He runs a hand over his forehead. "The two of us need to get back to set," he says, gesturing towards Jordan. "We need to duke it out over August some more." He tries a smile.

They both stand up. I follow them to the door, where Jordan stops, leaning against the frame.

The light is fading. I see the shadows across both of their faces. "What's done is done," Jordan says. "We can't change that."

"I know."

"But we also can't move forward like this." He exhales. "You think you're saving us by not choosing, but you're not. You're holding us here. I know we're supposed to say we'll be patient—I've seen the movies—" Jordan breaks off, shaking his head. "But until you act, Paige, no one is going to be able to move forward. And I just have to figure . . . I mean . . . that isn't what you want, is it?"

"Come on," Rainer says. He cocks his head and Jordan unhinges himself from the wall. They take off down the corridor.

I watch them disappear around the corner and when they're gone I'm filled with the biggest, deepest sense of loss. Because for the first time I realize I don't understand love at all. I thought it was sacrifice. I thought if I committed to Rainer when he needed me, if I refused to choose, if I let Jordan go, that that was love. But maybe love isn't about the things we give up. Maybe love is the thing that—after everything is gone—remains.

CHAPTER 19

The next morning I pull myself out of bed at five. The sun is still sleeping and I make my way, half conscious, into a bathing suit, grab a towel, and slide into sandals. My morning Maui ritual.

I pad down the pathway to the beach and sure enough, I'm met with that familiar calm at the water's edge. The soft lapping of the water, the moon passing the baton off to the sun.

I toss my shoes off, put my towel down, and when I sink my feet into the sand I instantly relax. The water is cool, but not freezing. It's early, and the sun is getting ready to rise—a sorbet sundae of color. As I swim, I let my thoughts spread out with the sky.

It feels like coming clean. Like I'm washing the last

six months off of me. With each stroke I let go a little bit more. I give it to the water. Greg's evil influence, I let it slide off of me. My sister's betrayal, I send down deep. The scandal with Jordan—it floats away on a wave. The photos and paparazzi and endless tabloids stories are no more than a drop out here. They seem silly, frivolous. Our lives, the minutiae of our celebrity, is no more than a blip on the radar of humanity. It doesn't matter. If I'm with Rainer or if I'm with Jordan or if I go back to Portland and start dating a customer from Trinkets N Things, it's irrelevant. We're insignificant, all of us. Just a speck on the face of one, tiny planet. And doggy paddling now, out in the great Pacific ocean, I have never felt so liberated by the realization of my own unimportance. I feel the weight fall off my shoulders right along with the water. I'm just one girl. I can't possibly be responsible for all that I think I am. Fulfilling the expectations of strangers is not in my job description. There's no way to make the whole world happy; it's just not possible. Responsibility isn't about pleasing others—it's about doing your best to be true to who YOU are, and letting people see that.

I've been so afraid of screwing up, letting people down, that I've made the greatest misstep of all: I haven't been *here*. I haven't paid attention. Because if I had been, if I hadn't been so busy being panicked over the press and my relationship and whatever image I'm projecting I would have seen what was right in front of my nose this whole time. I would have gotten it.

I'm just coming in when I see Jordan on the beach. This is his routine, too. Morning swims, sometimes surfing.

I swim up to the shore and jiggle the water out of my ears. He's a little ways down on the beach, and I grab my towel, wrapping it around me before heading over to him.

He's sitting with his elbows on his knees gazing out at the awakening horizon. He's not wet; he hasn't gone in yet.

"Hey," I say.

He looks up at me, confused, and then his face changes. "Good morning."

"Sorry," I say. "I didn't mean to interrupt."

"You're not."

He gestures to the sand beside him. I tuck my towel underneath me and sit.

"I've missed this," I say. I mean the ocean but Jordan leans over and chucks my shoulder with his.

"Me too," he says.

"You were right," I say.

I hear Jordan breathe next to me. "I've had a lot of opposing opinions lately, and I've been expressing them with embarrassing frequency. You may have to be more specific." He closes one eye and peers at me. It makes me crack up.

"Yesterday," I say. "The thing about us not being able to move forward."

"Ah." He leans back on his hands. "You think?"

"I do."

Jordan nods. "Okay. But I should have added something." He leans over and picks up a strand of my wet hair. He holds it between his thumb and forefinger.

"What's that?" I ask.

"You won't lose me," he says. "If you go back to Rainer, hell, if you move back to Portland. You won't lose me."

He tucks the hair behind my ear and I reach up and take his hand in mine.

"What about if I stay here and buy a beach shack and become a fisherwoman?"

"Especially then," he says, running his thumb over mine. He looks up at me and I see his eyes—black and bright. Like a comet through the night sky.

"Wouldn't that be awesome?" I ask him.

"Staying here?"

"Yeah. Just living off the ocean."

"We could," he says. He threads his fingers through mine. "We could renovate a small cottage."

"We have money," I remind him. "It may as well be a whole house."

"The success has gone to your head," he says, smiling. "Okay, a house."

"I'd decorate it with driftwood and shells and it would be all white and the windows would always be open."

"We'd have no doors," he says. "Just linen curtains."

I'm imagining this house. This cottage on the ocean. Jordan and I, living out our days in sunlit bliss. Feasting on fish and fruit and vegetables. Reading and sleeping and staying forever underneath the stars.

"Sounds familiar," I say.

Jordan quirks an eyebrow at me. "*Locked*?"

"Yes."

Jordan drops my hand and brushes his palms together. Some sand falls. "I've been thinking lately that I need to stop believing paradise is a hideaway. That the only way to be happy is to be somewhere no one can see me."

"Trying to tap into mainland Ed?" I joke.

"Maybe," he says. He's thoughtful for a moment. "I've watched you grow a lot," he says. "You're so much more comfortable being in this world than you used to be. You're not scared anymore."

"I don't know about that," I say. "But I'm trying."

He smiles at me. "I want that for myself."

"I want that for you, too."

"I'm sorry if I made you feel like it was more noble to hide." Jordan swallows. "I just didn't know any better. But now—"

"Yeah?"

We look at each other. Alone on the beach, the only sound our slight breathing and the waves crashing on the shore. "I don't believe that anymore."

"What changed?" I whisper.

"You have to ask?"

I feel my heart begin to hum. It's beating like it's powering not only my body but the whole goddamn universe.

"You," he tells me. "You changed everything. All of it."

"Paige!" I hear my name being called and whip around to see Jessica storming down the beach at a runner's sprint.

I scramble away from Jordan and stand up, my legs wobbly. "Slow down!" I call to her.

"Can't," she says. She reaches us panting. She sticks her hands on her knees. "Rehearsal. Starting. Early," she says. She straightens up and arches her back. "It is sad how winded I am right now."

"I just need five," I say. I look at Jordan. His expression is open and I want to tell him that he changed everything, too. That the world is entirely different because he's in it and that I've been looking at everything upside down and I want to see things rightside up, now. That I can.

"You're already ten late," Jessica says. "We gotta move. Jordan, your call time isn't until nine AM."

"Thanks, Jess," he says. "I'll see you guys later."

I'm about to follow Jessica when I feel Jordan loop his

pinky finger through mine. I remember the premiere—how he took hold of me the same way. Then it was our goodbye, but now it feels like something else. A promise, maybe.

And then he's picking up his surfboard and heading towards the water as I climb the path back to the condos.

I work mostly alone for the rest of the afternoon and wrap an hour after Rainer. Jordan is still on the sound stage rehearsing through a scene with Alfonso.

My phone rings on my way back up to the condos. It's Alexis. "Gorgeous!" she says before I have a chance to say anything. "I'm hopping an earlier flight."

"Alexis—I can't even believe—"

"We'll have plenty of time," she says. She sounds like she's on speakerphone. I hear the sounds of traffic. "Tell Rainer and Jordan to be at the airport at ten twenty with you."

"Alexis, we love you, but I highly doubt the three of us are going to voluntarily get in a car together."

"I just came out in front of the world," she says. "You can sit in the car with the two of them for twenty minutes."

"You're really gonna milk this, huh?" I say.

"Till it's dry. Tell them if they don't show up I'm holding a press conference to release all their secrets."

"I think they're already out."

"Darling," she says, "I've known those boys for ten

years in Hollywood. You are just the tip of the iceberg."

"We'll be there," I say.

"I know."

As promised, I get the three of us to the airport. I tell Rainer that Alexis had requested we all pick her up together and to my surprise, he's all about it. When we get to the lobby, Jordan is waiting for us.

"She called me," he says. "Shall we?"

Rainer's neon-blue convertible comes around and we all get in. Rainer drives, Jordan sits shotgun, me in the back.

I lean forward and fiddle with the radio and when Katy Perry comes on I leave it. Jordan tries to give me a hard time about it, but Rainer just turns it up. I catch his eye in the rearview and he winks at me.

Rainer has brought a lei and he hands it to me when we get out of the car. "You should give it to her," he says.

It smells like sugar and sunlight. These gorgeous yellow and white flowers. Plumerias and pikaki. My favorite Hawaii scents.

I loop the lei over my arm and walk behind Rainer and Jordan. Jordan points out an old, yellow Cadillac that is parked in front of baggage claim. "It's Rhonda," he says to Rainer.

Rainer shakes his head. I see him laugh. "God,

remember what a piece of shit that car was?"

"We asked a lot of it," Jordan says.

"That we did."

The two of them exchange a glance and I stay silent, walking behind. Their shared history, as Alexis reminded me, is extensive. Maybe she knows something about getting them back together that I don't.

We wait for Alexis where Rainer waited for me just a few days ago and she comes bounding down the stairs ten minutes later, the first one off the plane.

She leaps into Jordan's arms first. "Wilder," she says. "I missed you."

"Missed you, too," he tells her.

She looks radiant in ripped jeans, a loose white v-neck, and straw hat.

Alexis keeps an arm over Jordan and then slings one over Rainer. She draws them in so the three of them are in a huddle.

"Guys," she says. "I've invited you both to my homecoming to inform you that this rift of yours is over. I'm calling it."

Rainer leans back and raises an eyebrow at her.

"This is not up for discussion," Alexis says. "This is just a fact of life. I'm bored with this tension. Plus neither one of you ever fought over me like this, and frankly I find it kind of insulting."

"Clearly that would have been a lost cause," Rainer says.

"True," Alexis says. She squeezes Jordan's shoulder with her open palm. "Drop it," she says. "Now. Life is too short to not let the ones you love in."

To my complete shock, I see Jordan nod. "You're impossible," he tells her.

"Nothing is impossible," she says, untangling herself from them. "That's the point."

I see Rainer and Jordan exchange a conspiratorial glance.

"Now go get my bags," she says. "I have to talk to Paige."

Jordan laughs and starts walking towards the carousel with Rainer. "Good to have you back, A," he says.

"Don't forget it."

I'm marveling at them standing together waiting for Alexis's suitcases. They are *talking*. They appear to be *laughing*.

"How did you do that?" I ask Alexis. "Are you a witch?"

"Kind of," she says. "Paige." She loops her arm through mine. "I'm sorry I couldn't tell you the truth. You were dealing with so much already and it wasn't the right time."

I take her hand in mine. "You don't have anything to apologize for. You didn't owe me an explanation, you still don't."

She shakes her head. "I was worried about the wrong things—what it would do to my image and career."

"Hey I'm straight," I say. "And I still managed to massively screw up my image." She jabs me in the side and we both laugh.

"It's just time to come clean," she says. She keeps her eyes steady on me.

"I know," I say.

She nods. "Good."

The boys are waving to us from the carousel. "I'm assuming these giant Vuitton trunks are yours?" Rainer calls.

Alexis gives him a thumbs up.

They work together to lug the suitcases off the conveyor belt and each wheels one over to us. "Unless you have a small country coming down, I think we're good."

Alexis checks the bags. "Let's go."

We start off for the parking lot. The Cadillac is still there and Rainer and Jordan are reliving an extended Vegas weekend with "Rhonda."

"I told you eventually we'd be real friends," Alexis leans over and tells me.

"I never doubted it," I say.

"You did," she says. "But this is a night of forgiveness."

I squeeze her arm. "Thank you."

"For what?"

I gesture towards the boys. "This."

"That," she says, hiking her carry-on farther up her shoulder. "Has nothing to do with you. It never did. They just had to be reminded of that."

I help the guys load the suitcases into the car. We laugh as Alexis tries to be the architect of the whole thing. "What did you pack?" Jordan asks.

"None of your business," Alexis says.

Rainer holds the door open for us and we crawl in the backseat, Jordan up front. I'm thinking if there were cameras here now they'd catch the four of us joking and driving and singing to Taylor Swift. And there'd be no way to spin that as anything but the truth: four friends in Hawaii, catching up and moving on.

CHAPTER 20

We get Alexis settled. Jordan stays to hang out with her, and Rainer and I head back to our side of the condos. The last thing I hear when the door closes is Alexis asking Jordan if there is anywhere he can secure her frozen yogurt at this hour.

"This isn't New York City, A," Jordan says.

"Come on," Alexis says. "Since when do you not know how to make anything happen at any hour? That is not the Wilder I know and love."

"Fine," he says. "But you owe me."

Rainer shakes his head as the door snaps closed. "Walk you back?"

But Rainer's room is first, and when we get to his door he asks if I want to come in.

"Yeah," I say. I'm still wired from tonight, from having Alexis here. I'm not remotely tired.

Rainer holds the door open and he follows me inside. I go into the living room. Our condos are almost identical, but I've always thought he had the better view. I push the sliding doors open and step out onto the balcony.

The cool ocean breeze hits me and I lean over the railing, closing my eyes. "Today was pretty great," I say.

"Leave it to Alexis," Rainer says from behind me. "You were right, about Jordan and I."

"Which part?"

"All of it, I guess. I do care about him."

"I'm glad," I say.

"He's changed, you know." He clears his throat. "He's different now. I know a lot of that has to do with you."

"I don't . . ." I start.

"No," he says. He looks straight at me. "You do."

I turn away from the doorway and go inside. Rainer pivots to watch me. I take a seat on the couch where we've spent so much time—me in his lap, reading lines, kissing, becoming what we are.

"I keep thinking this is all going to make sense," I say. "That I'm just going to have the answer."

"Maybe that's not the point," he says. He's leaning against the sliding door, backlit by moonlight, and I'm struck once again by how beautiful he is. "Love doesn't have to make sense."

I look up at him. "Sit with me?"

He does.

I take his hand.

"You mean so much to me," I say. "In some ways more than anyone who I've ever known. Rainer, I owe you everything. I don't know who I am in this world without you by my side."

Rainer squeezes my hand. "That's not true anymore," he says. "We both know that."

I take a deep breath. "Maybe, maybe not. But I also know that we both have things to figure out still. I feel like we've been in this holding pattern for so long now. And I don't think either one us wants to be here anymore. You've been so patient with me, Rainer, but you shouldn't be." I inhale and force the next words out. "You need to let me go."

Rainer keeps tight to my hand. His tone is soft, not a trace of bitterness. "So you've made your choice, then."

"This isn't about Jordan," I say. "This is about us. You and me."

"I liked when there was a you and me." He smiles at me—it's small, sad, but still radiant. Still him.

"Me too," I say. "There still can be. Just not the way . . ."

"I want."

"I was going to say the way it used to be. Rainer, you have been so wonderful to me. You were the best boyfriend."

He snorts. "My track record would beg to differ."

"Not true. I'd never be where I am without you. Britney wouldn't, either."

He looks at me, but doesn't say anything.

"I know you feel responsible for her. But your dad's mistakes aren't your own. You can't hold up the world, Rainer. You're not superman."

"Well actually," he says, "I am."

"Real life, Rainer."

"Oh, right, that." He shrugs his shoulders at me.

"You need to forgive yourself for what happened," I say.

He exhales. When he speaks, it's quiet, reserved. "I don't think I know how."

"You'll learn," I say. "I'll help you."

He picks his gaze up to meet mine. "Tomorrow is our first day of filming," he says.

In the midst of Alexis' arrival I'd forgotten. He's right. We start *Locked in Love* in the morning.

"Thank you for being my Noah," I say.

"Always."

We sit side by side in silence. I hear the waves

crashing—irregular, unpredictable, and yet still eternal. Nothing can stop the ebb and flow of the tide, the pull of the undertow. It's a force bigger than anything we could hope to understand or control. Maybe love is the same way. Maybe Rainer is right—love doesn't have to make sense. The only thing I know for sure about love is that it does not die. I know because I've tried to kill it. I've tried and I've failed.

I touch the cowry shell at my neck. The one Rainer gave me all those months ago. Back when he was asking me to be his. And I know, in some ways, I always will be. We're August and Noah. He's the one she chose. Their story will live on far beyond us. We'll be together, somewhere, forever.

The next morning, five AM, I'm headed down to the hair and makeup suites. Sandy came in last night and I run into her in the lobby. She yawns and offers up her Starbucks cup in a wave. I signal back. I'm feeling good this morning, calm. Like the world is the way it's supposed to be. We're back where we're supposed to be. I'm hoping one thing in particular hasn't changed. And when I fling the door open, I see that I'm right.

"It's about time, honey girl," Lillianna says. She doesn't get up, she just holds out her arms, and I leap into them.

"You're here!" I yell.

"Of course, baby," Lillianna says. "I wouldn't desert you."

Lillianna has been working in hair and makeup in Hawaii for over sixty years. I spent every single day with her while filming the first *Locked*. Man, I've missed her.

She pats the chair. "Get in here," she says. "We got our work to do today. Have you used a brush since you left this island?"

"Barely."

Lillianna winks at me. "I know. I've seen the pictures. You and Jordan, huh?"

I shake my head. "You're already trying to get the dirt?"

"Honey if the sun ain't up, it doesn't count."

I think about my sister's tabloid confession, and I know, in the deepest part of my heart, that Lillianna would never do that. But I also can't bring myself to tell her what happened last night between Rainer and I. It feels precious, special—ours. I remember what Jordan told me on the beach so many months ago. That this life is hard, that the media will go in search of anything and everything. That you have to keep what's yours sacred.

Lillianna eyes me when I keep quiet. "Well if you're not going to dish the dirt, at least tell me what it's like being America's sweetheart."

"I'm hardly their sweetheart, and we both know that."

Lillianna grunts behind me, twisting my hair around

a curling iron. "That's your own fault," she says. "Why don't you give those cameras a flash of teeth?"

I twist around to look at her. She chucks my chin. "Lillianna, if you keep giving me unsolicited paparazzi advice I'm going to be late to set."

"Wouldn't be the first time," she says. But she unfolds her makeup bag and then she's putting on foundation with a small, wet brush.

"Did I ever tell you about the time Mr. Fred Astaire tried to win my hand?" she asks me. "I figure if you don't talk about your romantic life at least we can talk about mine."

I laugh. I never know if Lillianna's stories from old Hollywood are real, or not, but it actually doesn't matter. As I listen to her familiar, throaty voice fill me in on her romantic past, I can't help but feel at peace. A weight has been lifted this morning. I feel free for the first time in a long time. Like my life belongs to me alone.

I finish up with Lillianna and then head to the sound stage. Rainer is waiting when I get there. He's a different Noah at the end of this movie—cleaned up, transformed— and when I look at him it's almost like I'm seeing someone else entirely, someone new.

"Good morning," he says

"Hey."

He gives me a slow smile that seems to convey

everything I might possibly need to hear from him. *It will all be Okay.*

Jessica bounds over a moment later, holding out a cup of coffee. He takes it. "You're the best," he tells her. I see her grin at him and say something into her headset, scurrying off.

I look from Jessica to Rainer. And then I'm pushing past him to follow her to the craft service table.

"You want a cup?" she says, bobbing a tea bag into a mug.

I shake my head. "Jessica," I say. "Wyatt isn't back on this movie."

She looks around frantically before cracking a smile. "Wait, he's *not?*"

"We all love you," I say, "And we're so glad you're here. I just have to figure there is a reason you're not back with Wyatt on his next project." I think about Jessica at our press events, Jessica in Tokyo. Jessica back here, now.

She blushes. "I love these movies," she says, smoothing back her hair. "You know that."

I glance over my shoulder to see Rainer goofing around with the sound guys. I smile. I could see it.

"Yeah," I say. "I do."

"Isn't anyone working around here?"

I spin to see Sandy standing next to us. She's wearing, wait for it, an actual printed sundress. Blue flowers and all.

Color. I'm so stunned I'm speechless.

"What are you two chatting about?" she asks.

"Our once-director," I say quickly.

"Ah, Wyatt," Sandy says. "I prefer not to think of him as once so much as future."

"Is this about to get personal?" I ask her. Is she finally going to confess she and Wyatt are an item?

"For you, maybe," she says. She crosses her arms. "Guess who just signed on for *Closer to Heaven* and wants you for his leading lady?"

I gape at her. "Are you serious?"

"As a sunburn. You start directly after *Locked* wraps. Congrats, PG."

I jump and hug her. Jessica claps next to me. "Yay!" she says, bouncing on her toes.

"What's all the fuss?" Rainer asks, coming up to us.

"I got *Closer*, and Wyatt's directing," I tell him.

A wide smile breaks out on his face. "Nice," he says. We stand there, grinning at each other, until Alfonso comes onto the sound stage and calls us to begin.

I felt so out of place when I first got here. I was terrified one wrong move would send me straight back to Portland. But that's not true anymore. There is a solid center to this life, now. A core that is tangible and steady and unwavering.

This is where I belong. And just like I'm okay without Rainer, I'm also okay without Wyatt. I know August. She's a part of me. I can play her by heart.

Alexis and Jordan join us on set and Alfonso directs the four of us through our first scene. Like in rehearsals he's sharp, but he's also kind. I see his attention to detail is not the move of a control freak, but of someone deeply invested in a vision for this film. He wants what we all want: to make something spectacular.

Alfonso expects more from us because we can give him more. We're older, now. We're not the same people who came to this set over a year ago.

We've been to the MTV Movie Awards. We've traveled the world. We've fallen in love and gotten back up again. And, perhaps most importantly, we've seen these stories through. We know how they end, now. Who August chooses. I think she got it right, in the end. Maybe I will, too.

CHAPTER 21

The month flies by. It's so much fun having Alexis on set. She's silly and goofy, but beyond that she's a great actress. We play off each other easily and, man, does it feel nice to not be the newbie anymore. I like that I can be the one to help someone else through this massive movie.

I like that I know what time the sun rises and how to get Leilani who works craft service to pick up the good sticky buns (bribe her with Rainer time). I like that I know where the editing room is, how to get on Gillian's good side, and that you can never tell whether or not it's going to rain. I love that I know Rainer and Jordan's tells. That Rainer bounces on set when he's nervous or we're doing a big scene. That Jordan gets quiet, insular. That when he isn't talking it means he's thinking and he just wants to be left alone.

Alfonso is incredibly talented and the more we get to know him the more he reveals a warmth that Wyatt, despite how much I love him, never had. He's collaborative. I understand now that part of the reason he won't tell us exactly what to do is that he knows this movie is ours as much as it is his.

But it's only for a month. And then we're packing up. Rainer and Alexis back to L.A., and Jordan and I to Seattle. They'll be in and out of this shoot, but for the most part it's Jordan and I.

"I can't believe we're leaving already," I say at dinner on our last night. The four of us are out. Tourists have camera phones angled towards us, but from our favorite table at Longhi's, the one in the corner Rainer and I sat at together so long ago, they may be snapping photos of the ocean. "It feels like we just got back here."

"There is always movie three," Jordan says.

Rainer leans forward on his elbows. "Same place, different time."

"I just want to stay," Alexis says. She has a long white dress on (something she bought for me, and now exclusively wears), and she's sitting with her legs curled up under her. I admire her courage more than I could possibly ever tell her. It's true that the outside world has infiltrated our little island paradise. The press surrounding Alexis has been both radiant and condemning. They have applauded her bravery, but hammered her about lying and dating Jordan. Jordan is being cast, predictably, as a bad-boy runaway, scorned by both Alexis and me, not to mention the lingering Britney theories, and Greg and Rainer are still duking it out daily. Ironically, between the four of us, I currently have the best public persona. Nothing stays the same.

"Time to face the music, I guess," Alexis says.

Rainer puts a hand on her shoulder. "I'm with ya."

Jordan looks at me. For maybe the billionth time since that day on the beach I feel the anticipation rise up in my stomach like bubbles to the top of a champagne bottle. Ready to burst. All that is still to come. All the things we haven't yet said. What it will be like when it's just the two of us, the thing it feels like I've been waiting for forever.

Rainer checks his phone. "I gotta run," he says. He takes another sip of water and then motions for the waiter. "I got this," he says. "Sorry to jet."

"Last minute packing?" I ask.

I know Rainer is a terrible packer. On tour I used to do most of it for him.

He pushes his lips to the side. "Nah. That's what tomorrow is for. I said I'd meet Jessica for a drink." He gazes down at me. There is so much in his eyes. Tenderness. Forgiveness. Friendship. Love, too.

I smile. "Cool."

He leans down and kisses my cheek and for a moment Jordan and Alexis aren't there. It's just me and Rainer, redefining, re-figuring, ending up somewhere close to where we started.

"Jessica, huh?" Alexis says once he's gone.

I take a sip of iced tea. "Yeah," I say. "Jessica." It stings, a little, but so what. It's supposed to. I don't think you go from dating someone to having absolutely no feelings. The important thing is focusing on the ones that matter. Like being happy for him. I'm choosing to give that emotion more weight. And she's good for him. I see him calmer, happier, more himself. He's more authentic. He doesn't have to be a celebrity with her, and I think that's exactly what he needs. All this time Jordan and I have been figuring out how to be comfortable in the spotlight, what Rainer really needed was to figure out how to be comfortable out of it.

Alexis stretches. "Alright, kids," she says. "All of this doesn't come free. I need sleep."

I stand up and give her a hug. "I'll see you back in L.A.," I say.

"Don't unpack your swimsuit. We're spending every waking moment in Malibu."

I roll my eyes. "The more things change," I say.

"The more they stay at beach houses in the Colony." She leans close in to me. "Courage, young grasshopper," she says into my ear. And then, to Jordan. "Miss me daily."

"I'll do my best," he says.

We wave her off. "Fly safe," Jordan calls after her, but she already feels a million miles away. It's just us now. The air is tense; it crackles. I swear I can almost see it spark.

"Do you want to take a walk?" he asks me.

"Yes."

We head down to the beach. It's dark but the full moon has created a silver pattern on the sand.

"It's so beautiful here," I say.

"It is."

We're whispering. The night feels so still, so quiet, that if we spoke at volume our words would be carried away. And I don't want them to be, not this time. I want us to be exactly here now.

"Come on," Jordan says.

We start to walk. Past the place where I first saw Jordan, his back to me, taking in the ocean. Past the cabana where he first kissed me, the stretch of ocean where he saved my life when I got pulled out by the current during a morning swim. The same spot where Rainer rescued him a year later.

"Do you remember what you said to me that first day on the beach?" I ask him.

"When I saved you from drowning?" Jordan has a half-smile on his face. I see his eyes, his scar, his lips, all perfectly. It's like the spotlight of the moon is fixed on us alone. "Not really. Stuff about water safety, I hope. You didn't know a thing about the ocean."

"Not quite," I say. "You told me that there were things in my life the press was going to try to take away and that I had to work to not let that happen. You said I needed to protect what was sacred."

Jordan stops walking. He turns to me. "I guess that didn't really work out so well," he says. "They took Rainer from you, and your privacy, and—"

"Jordan." I'm edging closer to him. I can see the gold flecks in his eyes—like shooting stars in the darkness. "I didn't know what was sacred to me then, that was the whole point. But I do now."

"And?"

"You."

Jordan looks like he's going to speak, but I hold up my hand. I'm not done. I need to say this. All of it.

"For a really long time I avoided the way I feel about you. Because I didn't want to hurt Rainer and I didn't want to hurt some idea we've created in the world about who we are. I thought it would be too hard. But we're going to keep changing and just because we're doing it in front of so many people doesn't mean we don't get the same rights everyone else does. I don't want to live a lie, Jordan. Especially not with that many people watching. I want to be honest, with myself and everyone else." I take a deep breath. "The truth is that I love you. Underneath everything else, I love you."

"You love me?"

"Yes," I say. "You know that."

Jordan runs a hand over his chin. "You know we'd be followed by camera crews incessantly. They'd say you're fickle, that I betrayed my best friend . . ."

"Yeah?"

Jordan drops his hand. I see him looking at me with a smirk I recognize well. A little side-smile that tells me everything I need to know. That look on his face, it makes my heart feel like a creature all its own. That it could scramble straight out of my body if it wanted to, that's how alive it feels. "Most people would say that's reason enough not to be together."

"They're not us," I say. "I don't want to live my life based on some public idea of who I am. I want to live it based on what I want. And right now, Jordan, and since the moment that I met you, that's you."

"I see."

I cross my arms. "That's it? You *see*? That's all you have to say?" Have I been wrong about this last month? Thinking we were headed somewhere, that our ending up here was inevitable?

"That's all I have to say."

I open my mouth to start up again, to launch into more reasoning, to possibly yell, but my words are lost on his lips. He pulls me towards him and kisses me with an intensity that lifts me straight off my feet. In his arms, I'm flying. I see the beach below us. The million kernels of sand that used to be rocks, some billion years ago. I think, in the speck of space I have for thoughts with Jordan's hands in my hair like this, that everything changes, everything becomes something else. It's not our job to be true to who we were, it's our job to be true to who we are, right now. And if we don't allow ourselves this, this infinity of expansion, then we might as well not be alive at all. There is only one way to go in life, and that's up. Growth, evolution, *forward*. I want to keep moving.

"I love you, too," he says. "And I want to be with you. For as long as you'll have me."

Jordan takes my hand and leads me back to the condos and when he undresses me this time there is nothing separating us. Not what has happened, not even what will. I know we will change. I know we may not always feel the way we do right now. But I also know that none of that really matters. Because there is no way to predict life. If two years ago someone would have told me that I'd be August, that I'd be starring in *Locked*, that my face would be on the cover of *Vanity Fair* and that I'd be the number one Googled celebrity on the planet I would have never believed them. But that's just it. Life isn't meant to be believable. It's meant to be magical. Haven't you heard? Truth is stranger than fiction.

ACKNOWLEDGMENTS

A very special thanks . . .

To my incredible editor, Farrin Jacobs, for pushing me to make this the best book I could and for continuing to respect my vision for Paige, Rainer, and Jordan. You are the smartest. That's a word, right?

To my agent, Mollie Glick, for getting on board with whatever hair-brained scenario I'm coming up with next, and for letting me focus on this world, and its inhabitants, so completely the last few years.

To my friend and manager, Dan Farah, for the countless text messages, voicemails (mine) and emojis (only the calm ones). Thank you for challenging me to set the bar so unbelievably high, and for reminding me that all is well . . . most of the time.

To Tara Sonin, for teaching me how to be a boss, for taking care of me, and for allowing me to pay it forward the way I always dreamed I would, and could. Tara, I am so proud of you. Just remember: Gan Mao Ling.

To Rachel Petty, my wonderful UK editor, for your continued enthusiasm, brilliant guidance, and all-around awesomeness. I am so lucky to work with you.

To Leila Sales, for filling in whatever needs filling in in my life, whenever it needs filling in. I love you, wacky buddy. Thank you for your guidance and example and for letting me share this ever-evolving dream with you.

To Lexa Hillyer, for teaching me so much about what it means to be a woman and an artist. Lexa, I am proud of us, and how far we have come. May we continue to inspire each other with kindness and compassion (and Prosecco).

To Lisa Moraleda for being the best publicist ever and for putting all my crazy ideas in motion—this world is so much fun to explore with you.

To Tina McIntyre and Jane Lee for making Parker Witter live online. She appreciates it, even though she'd never say it :)

To Leslie Shumate for helping keep Paige in line on the page (and at LB).

To Janet Ringwood, friend and publicist extraordinaire. Thank you for being there for me always, for our wine-fueled afterlife discussions, and for reminding me to smile, and be present.

To Kat McKenna, UK fairy and marketing genius. Thanks for helping *Famous in Love* travel in such style.

To Hannah Brown Gordon, for continuing to be the best of the best.

To Liz Casal and Maggie Edkins, two of the world's greatest designers, for keeping *Famous in Love* looking smokin'.

To Brad Gendell, who knocks my novels to the top of his to-be-read pile every time there's a new one. As far as brothers-in-law go, I'd say I won the chosen jackpot.

To Guy, India and Fox Gendell for being my biggest (and littlest) champions. Watching you grow up is one of the great joys of my life.

And finally to my parents—I love you more today than yesterday but less than tomorrow.